The Blue Whale

PICAS SERIES 14

Canadä

Guernica Editions Inc. acknowledges the financial support of the Government of Canada through the Book Publishing Industry Development Program (BPIDP).
This publication was assisted by the Minister of Foreign Affaires (Government of Italy) through the Istituto Italiano di Cultura in Toronto (Director: Carlo Coen).

Stanislao Nievo

The Blue Whale

Translation and Afterword by Gaetano Rando

Guernica
Toronto·Buffalo·Lancaster (U.K.)
2000

Original title: *La Balena azzurra.*
First published by Mondadori, Milan, 1990.

Antonio D'Alfonso, editor
Guernica Editions Inc.
P.O. Box 117, Station P, Toronto (ON), Canada M5S 2S6
2250 Military Rd, Tonawanda, N.Y. 1415-6000 U.S.A.
Gazelle, Falcon House, Queen Square, Lancaster LA1 1RN U.K.

Typeset by Selina.
Printed in Canada.
Legal Deposit – Fourth Quarter.
National Library of Canada
Library of Congress Catalog Card Number: 00-107508
Canadian Cataloguing in Publication Data
Nievo, Stanislao
The blue whale
(Picas series ; 14)
Translation of: La balena azzurra.
ISBN 1-55071-118-0
I. Rando, Gaetano. II. Title. III. Series.
PQ4874.I4B313 2000 853'.914 C00-901134-X

Contents

1

"They talk under water. Ever tried doing it?"

"Under water? Once. I coughed, that's all."

"They don't. They keep their mouth shut like when we plug up our nose and lips and try to shout. You get a deep sort of sound."

"I've heard the dolphins make it."

"It's not quite the same with the whales. They use different frequencies and they use their stomach to help produce the sounds."

"They don't use their blowhole?"

"No, they don't display their emotions."

"They keep them to themselves?"

"Theirs is an internal communication."

"Do they talk?"

"You've got to be careful about these things. There's a wide variety of types. The sperm-whale, Moby Dick they call him, lashes out like a carpenter with his hammer."

"That's why they've sent me from Europe. To count hammer strokes and other variations."

"Yes, we asked for a statistician."

"Why not a zoologist?"

"No, better an outsider without any specific knowledge of zoology."

"What am I supposed to be investigating?"

"A herd of passing whales. They swim in and out of Trincomalee Bay."

"It's said they have some sort of intelligence."

"That hasn't been established yet. We don't know what sort of intelligence it is."

"I know so little about the subject."

"None of us know much about the blue whales."

"Blue whales?"

"We know less about them than about sperm-whales, and much less than dolphins. But to study them is far more fascinating."

"Nobody told me anything before I left to come here, to Colombo."

Miriam adjusted her position in the chair. The run-down office had huge yellow maps stuck on the walls. Outside lay the sun-drenched city. She had immediately fallen in love with this unkempt, impotent tropical city, set on the slightly wind-swept sea, its shores full of people. The day before, just after her arrival, she had gone for a walk on an outer harbour breakwater, not far from her hotel. In a crown of little artificial rocks she had come upon a lone fisherman talking to himself. Miriam didn't understand what he was saying but she supposed he was addressing his monologue to the waves and the fishes. It was a curious habit that she too sometimes practiced in secret: a conversation with wind and cliffs carried on in a language composed of whistling sounds. For her it had begun on a southern shore during a summer voyage. She had become aware of a strange ringing in her ear. The wind had insinuated itself like a whisper in that undulating call. A fleeting acoustic defect, perhaps a mysterious message from a different world.

She had experienced it repeatedly since then, and it had intensified her interest in matters of the sea. Later, when she was undertaking a statistical study on the oxygen consumption curve of dolphins in an aquarium she had thrown herself enthusiastically into the project and, on her own initiative, she had conducted a second study on the acoustic frequencies used by the cetaceans. It was the door to a different world which she had always sensed was there.

Miriam was a mathematician. For over a year she had

been filling in perforated diagrams for a veterinary research institute in Australia, her native land. Then she had accepted an unexpected job offer from a Third World aid agency and here she was on the island of Sri Lanka.

"You know what Sri Lanka is famous for?" asked the scientist who was briefing her on her new assignment.

"I don't," she replied.

"For serendipity."

"What's that?"

"The possibility of making unexpected felicitous discoveries while looking for something else. This island, full of unexpected revelations, was called *Serendib* by the Arabs."

"So?"

"In the middle ages the seafaring Arabs would say that Serendib was a magic place. An Englishman adopted the word as a scientific term. He called *serendipity* any type of unexpected discovery. Whales are serendipity."

The man fell silent, wrinkled his forehead. He was a tall Indian from Colombo, director of the NAS, National Aquatic System, research centre. He gazed at the woman, a determined look in his eyes.

"It's the biggest beast that ever lived, even bigger that the dinosaurs. There are a few thousand left scattered throughout the seven seas. They can grow to thirty metres in length. But it's difficult to approach them. They're shy. Here, on the eastern coast, a few come to Trincomalee Bay between the months of January and May, and they allow us to approach them. There's one especially that seems to want to communicate something. We want to study the phenomenon by gathering data on the acoustic frequencies. There's considerable progress to be made."

"How?"

"There are two projects currently under way. These

whales are an endangered species and we must do something."

"I understand."

"One of the projects is based at the mouth of the Saint Lawrence, a Canadian river which the whales visit every summer. They are shy silent creatures."

"And the other?"

"The other is the one you're involved in. Getting into the water here is quite pleasant, given a constant temperature of around 27 °, and the sea's exceptional transparency."

Miriam looked out beyond the orchid-filled veranda to the sun-drenched sea. The currents were marked by strips of emerald-tinted water. In the sky wild geese were flying in a row over light-fringed fishing boats. A seagull flew slowly past the lace curtains of the veranda window. The pylons carrying the electric wires gave out a vibrating sound. After a few moments that special sound in Miriam's ear returned, a siren echo.

"There's a herd of blue whales at Trincomalee," the man, sitting in front of her, went on.

"At this time of year?"

"Yes."

"Does the project involve observing them in the water?"

"In the water and from the coast."

"Don't know if I can do it. I'm a statistics expert. Sound recordings."

"You've had scuba diving experience?"

"Yes."

"Good. We'll give you every assistance, all the equipment you need."

"But I've only worked with dolphins in the pool."

"You'll see."

"What am I supposed to see?"

"We've sighted a huge female on several occasions. A beautiful blue whale twenty-seven metres long. She seems to display a certain amount of interest in women."

"That scares me a bit."

"She won't harm anyone. It depends if she likes the person. She's particularly interested in the Englishwoman who works with us. We've picked up very low frequency sounds on the hydrophones."

"How long has this been going on?"

"Since last year. We thought it was just a chance happening. But she's come back this year too, and has approached the Englishwoman again."

"Well, can't the Englishwoman carry out the tests? I'd rather work with the dolphins."

"The Englishwoman suffers from rheumatism. She can't go on."

"I get it."

"The whale's huge but quite docile."

"What has the Englishwoman recorded?"

"She'll play them to you herself at Trincomalee. The whales have an amazingly structured ear, an auditory channel just a few millimetres long set in a wax valve formed in concentric circles which ends in a bony bubble, strikingly similar to that of the human ear. A wondrous work of nature. It can stand pressures up to fifty atmospheres."

"But what are you looking for?"

"We're looking for the key to understand the language of the cetaceans."

"What can I do?"

"You've carried out observations on the emotional intensity system of dolphins. It's in your CV. That's the way to go."

"It was just a pilot study."

"Do a pilot study here too."

"But I did it on dolphins, in an aquarium. There's quite a difference!"

"It's your method that interests me. That's why I've asked you to come here, and we prefer a woman for the reasons I've just given."

"What equipment will you give me."

"A support vessel."

"Are they always peaceful? Couldn't they turn on someone who gets too close?"

"I don't think so. Of course, you can never be too sure of how things work out in the sea. But the whales have remained docile creatures, even though fifty or sixty years ago they were being slaughtered by the whalers in their thousands."

"Yes, but right there in the middle of the sea . . ."

"At NAS we believe that low frequency language is a key to a whole range of marine life we know nothing about. You're a statistics expert. I don't have to tell you about the law of numbers. At Valdes, in Argentina, someone's already managed to communicate with Right Whales. At Hawaii two dolphins communicate with Professor Herling. They possess a vocabulary of over fifty words and are able to compose hundreds of utterances."

"And at Trincomalee?"

"We're still somewhat behind. We study sperm-whales, dolphins."

Miriam's thoughts turned to the dolphins again. Increased oxygen consumption gave them a lucid, rapid intoxication. Their voice communicated something but she had not understood what it was. She had noticed only one thing: they seemed to laugh immediately afterwards. She guessed that mankind had lost something, an area of the brain had become dormant, domineered by the pressing development of other areas. It was difficult to listen to the language of nature, of its creatures. The sound she heard in her ear seemed a call from that world. She turned her head towards the veranda, half closing her eyes against the light.

Beyond the garden lay the sea in its blinding splendour. On one side large buildings formed a dusty grid separating the garden from a prison of urban cement. Out on the sea something leaped in a blaze of blue. She thought of the dolphins, wondered if they laughed, because they had stumbled on some unexpected solution to their problems. Were the men of the sea the most fortunate and free creatures on this planet? Was it down there that lay the key to unlock that mysterious world which she occasionally felt?

"Now we have our chance," the Indian went on. "The whales have a highly developed sense of family and of love. Every mother nursing a little one is accompanied by a female without child or who has lost one. They are the aunties. Sometimes they help the mother by suckling the young."

"How much milk does a little one take?"

"We don't know for this species. The sperm-whale drinks twenty kilos of milk a day, increasing constantly over a period of two years. So aunties and mothers help each other, changing roles in alternate years of pregnancy."

"Do the calves grow quickly?"

"In the first days they put on up to three kilos an hour."

"Do you know if they have any key sounds?"

"You could help us find out. You're a woman."

"How many of us are at NAS, at the coast base?"

"There's a custodian, Marta Hennes, the English scientist I've been telling you about, two sperm-whale experts and a fully equipped cutter with a three-man crew. Do you have any children?"

"No, why?"

"Mothers sometimes emit key sounds or words. The whale I've been telling you about has a child. We call her 'the mother' because we've always seen her with a calf."

The man was becoming increasingly wrapped up in this watery world. His interest sprang from his scientific work but seemed to go beyond and was much more intense. Miriam looked at him doubtfully. She essentially retained a statistics-based mental structure and traditional patterns of thinking. What she was hearing seemed to be an intricate mixture of intuitive spontaneity and scientific rigour that she found disconcerting. But she had only just arrived and everything seemed to form part of the picture. She ran her tongue over her lips a number of times, keeping her gaze downcast. She felt the man looking at her. She was beautiful and the world was her oyster. But even in matters like this statistics had taught her certain rules. She gave him a questioning look.

"I am somewhat puzzled," she confessed.

"I have to tell you one more thing. According to the theory, these whales seem to possess the ability to speak yet they love silence. It's a datum which makes you think. It demonstrates the importance of alternated sound and silence. It's been established that the structure of their receptive apparatus makes them capable of receiving a wide range of sounds emitted by animals, over great distances and in the worst type of turbulence. The sea is an immense loudspeaker."

"For those who have sensitive ears."

"At Trincomalee we have to extract something from the bottom of the sea."

"But aren't we actually looking for something else?"

"What?"

"The language of the sea."

"We must be careful not to confuse the issue. Each

species has its own method of communicating. The sea is an environment without a language of its own. It has laws, constants, that's all. We don't want to end up writing fairy tales. We're engaged in scientific research."

2

The lighthouse stood slim as a needle under the rain and the silence. From here you could make out the mouth of the Mahaweli River with its arms digging into Trincomalee Bay, the most important natural port in Asia. Under the rain-pocked surface of the bay lay the submarine canyon where plankton and shellfish attracted the whales.

The lighthouse was the only building on that white stretch of coast. It provided NAS with vertically placed sparsely furnished map-filled rooms. On the steps under the huge lantern Felipe the custodian, a fifty-year-old salt-encrusted devotee of the sea, was explaining to Miriam the view that could just be made out.

"The best times for the whales are at dawn and at dusk. Not today though."

Felipe was a *burger* of Portuguese origin. Thick-set, black eyes, sparse beard under black hair, ears frayed by an open-air life, he spoke several languages, all badly but with precise terms. He read the sea like an open book. He turned, and looked at Miriam.

"The lighthouse is the reference point for the whales," he said pointing to a far-off shape which Miriam was not able to identify.

"They come in family units."

The rain was drawing away in gusts, tracing arabesque patterns on the windows of the room.

"They come right under here to leap and play," Felipe

explained. "They're here even now, four of them at least. But *she's* not there."

She was the huge female they had been discussing, the women's friend. The rain dragged on like Felipe's monologues, gusts alternating with sunlight bursting through the clouds. The man was an expert on birds and Buddhist legends. He had been living at the lighthouse for many years with a Tamil assistant. Felipe turned around and picked up a pair of binoculars.

A row of pilot books covered the bottom of the observatory where a considerable variety of objects – rolled-up papers, tools, boxes and a hotplate for making coffee – were arranged on shelves placed in a semi-circle.

A black youth came in. Miriam had already met him.

"This is Luis," said Felipe, "my assistant. He lives here with his wife Dipika. There's also Marta, whom you've met."

Marta was the English scientist who worked for NAS, a touchy, reserved woman of indefinable age. They all lived above each other, a flight up or down. Vichi, a short lame man who looked after the cleaning, lived at the bottom of the heap. It was a vertical world.

Miriam quickly found her bearings, accepting the rules of the small community. The first was to never miss the passage of the whales and to identify them by photographs of tails and fins. The rainy days were followed by scorching-hot ones with crystal-blue skies.

"Today is a blue day ideal for blue whales," said Dipika one morning.

She leant her head to one side, sweetly. In the room half way up the lighthouse the Sinhalese woman was putting on make-up, inviting her friend to follow suit.

"Where's Marta?" asked Miriam.

Dipika looked up to indicate the observatory, keeping her eyebrows raised longer than necessary. Marta was reserved, touchy, hard-working, Dipika was, by contrast, cheerful, chatty and Miriam preferred her. She had an oval-shaped face with large attractive eyes. In front of the mirror she adjusted her long batik skirt.

"This cloth never changes, but we change inside."

Miriam had little opportunity for a tèête-à-tête with her. She asked a thousand questions to which Dipika gave ironic replies. They gossiped for a while. Luis was a compulsive cook, Marta was obsessed with teaching. Miriam asked if Felipe had a family.

"Who can stand him with that character of his? Only a lighthouse if it's tall enough and you don't see him all that often. Sometimes he's full of life and at other times he doesn't utter a word for days. He just loves dolphins. You'll soon see."

One evening, a few days later, it happened.

"The sea's a strange sort of place," said Felipe as he sat down to the evening meal and began telling a fishing tale. "Just as well there's the dolphins."

He went on to make a series of comments which caused Miriam to laugh, staring at her like a cat.

Felipe indicated a worn nautical map of the world hanging on the wall, his finger pointing at New Zealand.

"We met them here in 1970. Thousands and thousands of animals – they covered an area twelve miles long by three quarters wide, I reckon. As if the whole city of Colombo had been invaded by dolphins. A really impressive noise. We couldn't say a thing, just look, glued to the gunwales. They never touched the ship – as if it wasn't there. Like a floating carpet, they were. A sailor lowered himself down a rope to walk over them. Crazy!"

Miriam shut her eyes. She saw the scene and imagined the water which had been transformed into fish, and singing dolphins into wind. She imagined Felipe shouting and climbing on some part of the boat as he witnessed the scene.

"A merry army," commented Felipe. "I wasn't just the fish that were crazy. All of us were; men and dolphins in the middle of the sea."

He began to sob sweetly. It was his way of laughing. His throat, covered with short grizzled hair, made you think of the skin of an animal full of pins in a taxidermist's workshop. Felipe was a fine-looking animal, a cunning look about him like that of a dolphin, his smile always readily radiant.

"On the high seas, that's where you've got to go, people of few years! That's where the future lies, oh you scientists eager for numbers and sighs! Take there your magnificent machines which analyse the void."

"So we must go away?" joked Dipika. "But this is our home."

Miriam joined in.

"Did you really see the city of the dolphins?"

"For three whole days."

"Did anyone write a report?"

Felipe shrugged his shoulders.

"That's your world, papers and numbers. I'm on the other side, the side of the sea. Why don't you go and dive in instead of counting how many time the fish leap?"

He wanted the girl. He went on telling stories, some true, some made up. The wind has risen in the limped moonlit evening.

"Once upon a time something happened here too, at the end of a moonlit night. One day in May, at dawn, when the little ones are born and the sea is like oil, a female came right up to the lighthouse. She was a dolphin and had difficulty swimming. I noticed that the baby was half out of her belly, you could see its head. It's dangerous when the head's out like that – if the mother turns the baby inhales water and drowns. She had noticed this, kept her belly turned up and was calling for help by uttering whistling sounds. Seven dolphins came – I could see them clearly from up here – they formed a circle around the mother supporting her head and tail with their snouts."

"What happened then?"

"All of a sudden the baby slipped out and swam away. He had made it. They supported him so he could breathe. He listed, turned over, but they put him right side up like you do with a child who topples over. They formed a circle and went off with the baby in the middle."

Shortly after they finished the meal. Dipika cleared up, Felipe went up to the light followed by Miriam.

"Have you ever seen that whale, the one that's always around here?" She asked.

Felipe looked at her closely. Miriam felt his desire.

"I can tell you how whales and dolphins make love, if you want."

Miriam looked into his eyes, shrinking away a little. A mischievous impulse prompted her to respond.

"Do they do it like we do?"

"We've never done it, you and I. But I can show you how they act, which is very lovely," he said gracefully.

Miriam laughed nervously, her eyes shining.

"Here's how it goes," said Felipe.

With graceful gestures he imitated the male dolphin swimming around the female. Miriam looked on from her perch on the steps. Felipe climbed up a few steps making strange twittering sounds, then climbed down again. "The dolphin's love play is a carousel of close passes." He raised a hand as though to touch her at a distance so that Miriam could touch him if she wanted. She did not move. Felipe came a little closer.

"The males score if they reassure the female and amuse her with the sounds and snorts they utter."

He bent almost as if he were dancing the tango. Miriam watched silently while he hummed a whining sort of tune. Through his open shirt his chest looked like that of a silvery marine creature.

"Is that the dolphin's love song?" she asked unembarrassed.

Felipe smiled and climbed nearer. He took her hand ever so gently, holding it in a wave-like motion without tightening. Then he let it go, circling round the stairs with heavy sighs. Miriam watched fascinated. She felt as though she were swimming in the sea with someone telling her tales of love. She held out her hands to Felipe and he came near, repeating the pantomime without touching her. She descended, hands still outstretched, imitating his gestures. They circled each other as if swimming. She danced caressing his hair while he gently guided her.

"The dolphins like to make love with all creatures. It's a way of life with them and they try it every chance they get, sometimes even with herrings. It's a sort of love which is partly maternal, partly sensual. It comes and goes merrily."

"Will we too?"

They laughed continuing their dance, alternately caressing and pushing each other away until they could no longer stop their carousel.

"I'll take you out to sea, you'll see how lovely it is," said Felipe.

3

For millennia the sea of Sri Lanka has attracted the desire of far-away men. King Solomon had sent his vessels here and on these shores Campanella had dreamt the City of the Sun. In the hinterland four religions identify the same mountain with their great founding fathers, from Adam to Shiva, from Bhudda to Thomas. Here, according to tradition, Jonah had fled from God and from the whale. In the warm waters of Trincomalee Bay, where the whales come to meet with man more than in any other place in the world, natural history intertwines with the divine.

The whales come from the antarctic seas for the breeding season. Between these shores and the icy wastes of the south there is no land, only the ocean which tumultuously breaks ashore here after thousands of leagues. Lighthouses keep vigil on the cove-punctuated shores rotating like the eyes of a falcon.

Miriam watched the racing dolphins from the lighthouse while the custodian told her a thousand tales. These were thrillingly intense days. Rules and barriers had dissolved, the inhabitants of the lighthouse were rendered speechless by the force of that spectacle. Felipe's telescope helped Miriam find traces of life under the coast. Statistical tables were carefully compiled but they were only the threshold to the explosion of desire. These strange and unusual circumstances kindled in Miriam a sexual tension she had never experienced which was unleashed by Felipe's alternating shyness. At night Miriam dreamt of dolphins. One of them held her tight, dragging her into a whirlpool while she tried to catch hold, powerless in its grip. She looked for Felipe but could not see him. Hot hooks ripped her face, her legs.

She averted her eyes as the creature which held her in its strong grip violently possessed her, the siren call of a marine fury. She let herself go as Felipe washed over her, a wave which came to rest like a wreck in front of the lighthouse.

For two days she stayed alone not even going down for meals. Instead, she went down to the lowest line of rocks swept by the waves. The dolphins had gone. Iridescent patches reminded her of the force of desire. She hated that story and the cunning fury of the custodian. Her agitation turned into a desire to dive deep into the sea. All things here transmitted a feeling of happiness, peace, instinct. The whales must certainly feel something – that's why they had chosen this place for breeding and for their contacts with man. For a long time she gazed at the surface of the sea until her eyes hurt.

As she made her way beck to the lighthouse the sound returned in her ear, that whistling sound which had been obsessing her since she had left her country. She welcomed it like a friend. In the evening she went down to the dining room, determined to face the others. She rushed in, flinging the door open. Only Luis was there. They spoke of a machine that needed fixing and of a long-expected letter he had just received. Miriam asked after Felipe. Luis avoided looking at her directly.

"He's gone. Didn't he tell you?"

Miriam nodded to soften the blow, learning that Felipe would be away for at least a week. She angrily threw herself on her meal. Dipika and Marta came in a moment later.

Marta, more touchy and reserved than usual, was immediately plied with a whole range of technical questions related to the project and was obliged to reply. They continued the discussion, mentioning Felipe, and Miriam manipulated the topic slipping in and out of the conversation. But it was Dipika who really got down to the heart of the matter after a pregnant silence.

"He's different from the rest of us," she said. "If he doesn't come back you'll go and look for him."

Miriam laughed: "I still have to record three sets of observations before the end of the month and the big herds should be arriving in the next few days. There's lots to do."

The dolphins would be coming with mothers and little ones swimming close to the old white-streaked males skilled in the ways of a migration unchanged since prehistoric times, in search of squid and cuttlefish which the Mahaweli river brought down to the sea.

Uneventful days followed. The long waves swept slowly in the right direction, as if in a parade, but the fish did not appear. Plankton and diatom formed a saline broth over thousands of hectares of sea. It looked like dirt and rubbish, but was, instead, the nucleus of the origin of life. It was the beginning of April.

Miriam set up a new observation post on the other side of Trincomalee Bay, at Swami Rock beyond Fort Frederick, a rocky niche set on a perpendicular spur. The waters below flowed in slow-moving whirlpools. Her anxiety for the arrival of the dolphins mixed with desire for the return of Felipe. For hours on end she would stay glued to the binoculars. Right to the horizon only the odd boat floating on an empty sea; there were no dolphins in sight.

Raising her head, Miriam saw the seagulls greeting her in widely-spiraling flight, as they did every afternoon at the same time. One of them had a spotted wing. Miriam recognized it and took pleasure in following its flight. The bird dived. Miriam lowered the binoculars which got caught up in the strap so that in untangling them she lost sight of the seagull. She began looking for it but her search came to a sudden stop: less than fifty metres away a huge head was rising out of the sea. The mouth, covered by a thick layer of bubbles, appeared to be laughing. An island appearing out of the depths, it blew out a column of air tall as a cypress tree and arched ponderously.

Miriam watched. She looked for the eyes and found one hooded in wrinkles at the corner of the mouth. It was still and seemed to be staring at her, attracted like a magnet. It disappeared and reappeared as the creature rolled slowly like an overturned ship with its keel upwards before descending into the abyss. It was an imposing being which made everything else look small. The head sank below the surface and, in its wake, the coils of a very long, ever rotating, hardly recognizable animal rose and vanished.

The strange form rotated again and again, until it raised a huge tail which disappeared without a sound. It came from a world Miriam had dreamed of. The dolphins were its merry ambassadors but there, before her, was the queen, risen from the depths like a prehistoric monster. It swam forwards, dragging on the surface eyes which seemed to laugh with crushing sweetness. The huge creature threw up a column of water, spun around itself, raised its short fin and continued to spin like an island gone mad. The tail arched, raising a column of water, a gust of wind which dissolved in the sound in Miriam's ear, suddenly becoming very acute. Everything disappeared in a perfect whirlpool of bubbles. The sea remained empty.

"The mother!" Shouted Luis from the lighthouse. "She's back, she's back."

4

Miriam jumped out of the boat into the water. It was pleasantly warm and she swam for a minute around the vessel, relaxing. Then she dragged out the microphone hanging over the side; the lead ran freely under the surface. She pulled the mask over her face and looked around: a small swarm of silvery fish was swimming away from her in the blue water; in front of her a black shape rising turned out to be a tuna. The marine spectacle moved slowly, lit up by the sun. A momentary current caught the woman in its whirl. It was warm and still. Miriam began swimming again, diving down a metre or so. The microphone followed her down, its arched wire forming a question mark. Blue opened out around the swimming body and the ocean floor vanished completely. Miriam did an about turn, held on to the boat, got her breath back and went off again.

The water was clearer near the surface. Below, it took on an ever deeper hue, with the sun's rays concentrated around Miriam's shadow almost as if supporting her. A squid appeared, a black-ringed theatrical mask, its ridiculous head preceded by dancing tentacles. The eyes of the beast were on Miriam as it passed her waving flexible banners and disappeared. The woman turned her head and saw only blue above and below.

She was afraid. Only pride kept her down there. The cetaceans were below; a kingdom without boundaries, compared to human dimensions. A shiver ran along her spine again, fear and pride, pride and fear, curiosity, courage, the cold of long insistent breathing, sudden heat, trembling, and again spasmodic cold fear. Miriam could understand why Marta had given up diving after several weeks. She forced her eyes to look beyond the sun's rays to where all was blue: what if some black, enormous shape were to come out? She was both exhilarated and exhausted. She directed her gaze at a point, a fish, but it darted away. Every sign of life had vanished. Perhaps the animals felt something huge approaching. This was the whale's domain, in front of Trincomalee Bay. That's why the boat was there. Miriam had not wanted anyone else with her in the water, she desired to face the situation immediately. She was good in the sea and the recurrent fight against fear was an old problem of hers which she preferred to solve on her own.

She heard the boat's siren. They were calling her. Her head broke surface. On board, Marta was making frantic signals. Miriam raced for the boat which was about thirty metres away. A huge shadow settled close to her. A cloud, she thought. She increased her speed and at the same time turned round. Nothing, only a silent foamless undertow. The boat was heading towards her. The shadow came back. Miriam turned round noting the squid fleeing in a cloud of ink. The black shadow advanced through the folds of blue, covering her. For a split second she felt oblivion, her end coming in the black all-enclosing water. She moved her arms frantically, breaking out of the black cocoon, out of the womb of darkness towards the sun-lit boat. The shadow was pursuing her in thick spirals but two huge warm hands suddenly pulled her out of the water. She was hoisted on board, dripping, the dark dissolving. A little stunned, she joined in the general burst of laughter.

"Beginner's luck!" shouted a man's voice.

The boat pushed its motor to the limit. It was a thirty-year-old cutter, a military vessel refurbished for fishing. It tacked towards the coast.

"It appears six times in the Bible. Did you like it, Miriam?" said the helmsman who had spoken before.

"I saw nothing, only black, darkness."

"It was the *lewn-tan,* the beast who is the denizen of the deep, the leviathan. Didn't you see it? It's been hiding down there since the times of Jonah and Isaiah. They too tell about it."

"But what is it?" stammered Miriam.

"A sperm-whale," replied the helmsman. "You're lucky. You met it right away, first time out at sea. It's a female. We recorded her greeting – toc-toc, toc-toc – she was chatting with you."

"I didn't hear anything."

"The hydrophones picked it up."

Miriam was astonished; her teeth chattered with the cold. With a harsh feeling in her throat, her hands a violet colour, she watched the smooth sea. Her feet were blackened as if they had been burnt.

"The kiss of the depths," said Marta ironically. She was sitting on the bow in the sun.

"Watch out next time," said the Sinhalese helmsman who was commander of the cutter and knew everything about the Bible.

"How come I didn't see it?"

"They just come up like this," the man went on. "The sea is full of crustaceans brought by the river and that attracts the sperm-whales. Then they cruise back and forth, up and down."

"But did it pass behind the boat?"

"It came from the open sea. It often happens."

Miriam sat on the deck, caught her breath. She asked about the blue whale, the one at the lighthouse.

"It wasn't her. But it's a good year. You've brought us luck."

"You're a *Manaisa,*" said the youngest sailor, Anthony.

"What's that?"

"It's a sort of piper who plays a magic instrument and

makes the animals come out, a character from the local mythology," said the helmsman.

He got Anthony to take over the tiller and went down into the cabin to turn on the radio. Miriam started following him but an arm stopped her. Marta wanted her to get back to work – what had just happened was a usual enough event. Then she put the headphones on again and listened to the sounds picked up by the hydrophones. She was all huddled up in a jumper, her bare legs sticking out, lips nervously quivering. The waves were rocking the boat.

"There's not a thing to be heard," said Marta loudly. "It had shown its tail a couple of times before. When it passed close to you the sperm-whale was quite calm."

"How do you know?" asked Miriam.

"From the way it lifted its tail."

The second sailor, in the stern, jumped up, his hand shading his eyes.

"Moby Dick!" he shouted. "Nine o'clock."

Everyone looked in the direction indicated by the figure nine on a clock dial. About forty metres away an oblong trunk was blowing towards the sky. It was the sperm-whale.

"It's a female," said the sailor. "It's coming."

Marta passed the binoculars to her companion and together they watched. Against the light the cetacean looked like a huge rock, without any of the sinuosity of an animal. Miriam leant against the mast and looked at the ocean, that world of alternate light, in a continuity which defied any sort of comparison. The binoculars ranged under the water line. An infinity of different life forms lay down there and the cetacean belonged to that world even though it had to come up to the surface to breathe.

Miriam let herself go and whispered to Marta who continued to watch through the binoculars.

"Measure the distance and mark it as soon as it moves," she replied coldly.

Again Miriam heard that whistling sound in her ear. The sperm-whale opened its mouth towards the sky and gnashed its teeth. The frequency of the sound modulated as the dark cetacean repeatedly hit the water. Miriam turned to Marta but did not dare interrupt her since she was completely absorbed, observing through the binoculars. She shook her head to loosen her hair which had closed round over her ears due to a series of hardly perceptible vibrations. The roll of the cutter was beginning to get to her.

"I'm drunk," she said to herself.

Marta shook her, telling her again to take the measurements but at first Miriam couldn't understand. She was supposed to note the times when the whale appeared and disappeared. Now there were two of them, the other was approaching as the cutter tacked. Marta handed her a camera but Miriam did not take it.

"Are you asleep?" she hissed at her slowly.

Miriam was grateful for that little bit of understanding. She took the camera and began to operate it. On the surface the whales were leaping in a line. She stopped and began to follow the cetaceans which were re-emerging like rolling tree trunks. One gave an enormous burp which dissipated in the air. Everyone laughed.

The whales dived, tails up, coming back up to the surface after about twenty seconds, their heads floating like enormous corks. They headed for the cutter, two powerful machines rising from the sands of time. The blow-holes on top of their heads looked like crooked smoking cones. Marta recorded the sounds, the men handled the boat, talking excitedly. Miriam did nothing.

The sound in her ear had become an exciting whisper. Ten metres away, you could see great quantities of seaweed and crustaceans grappled to the backs of the animals whose long bodies were like submarines.

"Don't make a sound," whispered the captain.

The women had stopped working and were gripping the braces. The whales stood still. It was a couple, the female had a hairy hump half way along her body, the male had his blow-hole to the left. They looked like just-emerged volcanic islands.

The male lifted its head opening its saw-like jaws again. Ivory teeth shone, then everything tipped over as the tail went up. Miriam felt a stab of pain. The whistling sound had disappeared, changing into the rhythm of a moving train. Uneasiness took hold of her. The whales diving into the water one after the other shone in the blue, companions in an eternal holiday to which Miriam felt the desire to return. The crew was standing still, their eyes on the disappearing cetaceans, observing even the smallest detail. The clicking of Marta's camera replied to the toc-toc emitted by the whales. As soon as they disappeared, Miriam's ear returned to normal.

There was a sound like a waterfall. The cutter rolled half over while everyone grabbed hold of the violently shaking boat. A third whale had appeared, very close. Miriam tipsily leaned out in an attempt to touch its tail. The captain grabbed her, pulling her back, then rushed to the bridge while the two sailors inspected the bulwarks. The three turned, looking at each other and smiling at the women as the last of the whales vanished below the blue water. Marta ran below deck to the hydrophones. Miriam sat down exhausted.

"It's love play," said the captain.

"Will they come back?"

"Will the lovers return?" echoed the other.

Miriam wanted to add something, but wasn't quite able to articulate it. She was strangely jealous as though she had been left out of a game to which she belonged. She thought of Felipe but banished his image, instinctively transfering her concentration to the blue whale sighted at the lighthouse. But *she* had not appeared and Miriam once again felt bitterly disappointed, even though she had just witnessed a most remarkable spectacle.

5

Three sperm-whales in a row were heading towards the women swimming in the rosy light of morning. Like a puffing black train arriving from an unknown place, the convoy stopped where the two women were passing. Marta held Miriam tightly as she did not know what to do and felt her fear returning. In her head the hammering sounds were like a mysterious code that appeared to be telling her something.

A baby sperm-whale appeared from behind the adults, approaching his mother's breast with a half-open mouth, biting the water in liquid play. Ten metres away Miriam was swimming so as to keep her distance with Marta at her heels. Marta grabbed hold of Miriam in a shiver of terror. Miriam hit out at her to free herself but swallowed fear and water. She felt a sort of fatalism which always follows fear in marine encounters. The whales were motionless, rotating their little eyes. Miriam could see the baby's teeth, a long pincer-like saw: through it the baby whale was trying to familiarize itself with the new world it had just entered.

The mouth opened in a pointed shape under the

head; inside it a rough shape snaked, beating the water until it became murky. The women retreated.

When the water cleared again the baby had drawn away, a blue-eyed piece of wood distractedly gasping in front of its mother and another huge whale.

Miriam remained still, Marta just behind her. Fish of all sizes swam round the whale mass like busy servants. The cetaceans looked like gods of the underworld, their clear eyes restrainedly rotating with liquid force. Miriam watched, motionless on the surface of the water.

The baby approached the mother searching out the nipple and ran into a milky fluid. The whole convoy disappeared together with the satellite fish and the water remained empty. The encounter had lasted five minutes.

Several eventless days passed. The hydrophones picked up signals, soundings of unidentifiable animals, communications between individuals which did not make an appearance. Above the surface the sea took on a whitish colour under a sky covered with a thin layer of clouds. It was the middle of April.

The two women went into the sea twice a day, at dawn and at dusk, together with Alex, an Indian photographer. The three man crew remained on board.

The three in the water encouraged each other, saying that encounters in the sea were always peaceful. At most, the cetaceans disappeared unexpectedly, without any violent motion. They couldn't understand why.

The two women had come to an agreement. The presence of a companion in the water was reassuring for both. It was an ambivalent female move. When they returned to the cutter, the crew lifted them bodily out of the water. They often reacted by trembling all over, a reaction caused by the proximity to the huge sperm-whales.

"Their head is full of sperm, *spermaceti,* it's called.

Sperm that turns into oil. It gives tremendous vitality," Anthony was saying as he hoisted the swimmers out of the water.

"They are leviathans, animals in a pure state," said the captain from the bow. "They come and go as they please. They lead a double life, I reckon."

Anthony went up to Marta and helped her take off her wet suit. Then he turned to Miriam.

"I owe part of my life to one of them."

He told that when he was working on a whaler he had been abandoned at sea after having fallen overboard unnoticed by his companions. A sperm-whale had pushed him towards the coast. From that moment he had stopped hunting those great creatures of the depths and had never gone back to sea.

"But what do you think when you hear those knocking sounds they make on the hydrophones?" asked Miriam.

"I don't really know. We study them like you study animals, but they are a phenomenon of nature, like the wind, like the rain."

Anthony went off to secure two grappling-irons which had come loose. He came back, taking a small book out of his pocket. The women looked at him, questioning.

"It's a poem."

"How come you're showing it to us?"

"Listening to the whales is like listening to the wind, I told you. An occupation for meteorologists and poets. It's a far-away world."

"But the cetaceans saved you. They're more substantial than the wind."

"So's poetry." He went on leafing through the book in his hand. "I can't find it. It's a poem about a woman and a whale."

"Really? I'd like to know what the oriental poets think of whales."

"There's many tales told here."

"Sea, darkness, monsters are popular everywhere," said Miriam. "Are there poems like that in the book?"

"There's a poem by a Trincomalee fisherman: he's blinded by the sun while out fishing and tries to make it back to shore. It's difficult to translate but it goes something like this: 'At the blowing of the round wind the eyes come adrift and the sun sucks them out. But a third eye is set in place, an additional one, a poet's ear which listens to the men of the sea, the great ones who speak by beating on the water.' "

Anthony stopped speaking and smiled.

"Go on."

Anthony kept smiling, embarrassed.

"Shut your eyes and listen," he said. "Melville said they were monsters, but it isn't true. Even today we shout 'Moby Dick, Moby Dick!' when one appears. No one says *spermaceti* or sperm-whales. But who can understand what the whales say?"

The cutter traveled on as the sun, close to the horizon, became warmer. A fishing boat shone in the distance. An acute beating sound came from an unidentifiable direction and a whistle interrupted the conversation. Marta lowered the frequency band and resumed marking the graph. It was hot in the cabin, the wood gave out an intense odour. Miriam looked in to ask for an explanation and Marta told her about the presence of the cetaceans. Miriam looked over the side. Below, a dozen or so metres away, the sea bottom vanished in darkness. The woman raised her head and picked up the binoculars. An enormous round shape boiled on the flat ocean.

"The daisy," muttered Marta.

The whales had formed a circle on the surface around

a female in trouble. It was a pattern which the cetaceans sometimes formed on the high seas. The strange flower sparkled with foam over a length of fifty metres. A distaff-shaped column of spray rose from it.

"Blue whales," said the captain. "See how they blow."

The whistling sound in Miriam's ear grew rapidly in intensity. On the water the petals of the daisy lifted. Miriam lost all sense of what she was doing. Like a robot she put on mask and flippers and jumped in. The whistling sound disappeared. She felt a tightening in her stomach, her shoulders became very hot. For the first time she felt fear disappearing into the blue water like a black fish.

She went down a few metres, felt the pressure and came up again. Nothing appeared on the horizon but beyond were the whales. The blue water had become a challenge; it gave out a cold sensuality. Miriam's face was burning. The sun was holding her up with ribbons of light which irradiated everywhere. She felt like a merry marionette in the hands of a hidden puppeteer. The whistling sound came back, shyly, distantly. She merged the sound with the blue and it felt as though she were in a film. Behind her she saw Alex with his camera, the only non marine reality, a benevolent stranger more than a companion. The other sailor, Puck, and then Marta, joined Alex. They surrounded Miriam, forming a miniature daisy in an attempt to drag her back. It was the same thing the whales were doing, circumventing fear and transforming it into a lifebuoy for their comrade in trouble. But to communicate one needed to go beyond the daisy formation.

Miriam separated from her companions, swimming in search of the liquid peace which marked the beginning of a different reality. This gave her a sense of belonging, shedding the last vestiges of apprehension. The whistling sound came and went, a monologue of detached utterances, a little bird without body, sweet and empty. It burrowed through the brain, changing the stroke of the swimmer. The woman's chest was heaving. The whistling sound became fainter, then faded away. Miriam turned to look for her companions. She saw them fleeing like frightened frogs. She turned again and the sun was blotted out by a huge shadow which blended with the whistling sound returning. It plunged into an abyss of sound; she was transfixed by syllables she did not understand, a strange alphabet. The whale was calling her. She froze. An eye passed close to her, soundlessly cunning.

"Let her go on but keep an eye on her," said the captain to the three who had returned to the boat.

"If there isn't a baby about to make the mother nervous, this could be our main chance," said Marta as she was rubbing herself dry.

The daisy formed by the whales pulsated in the sea. The whale in the middle was regaining its strength and the others slowly attempted to drag it away. Miriam could make out their enormous bulks in the water. She swam in circles between the blue of the sea and the more intense blue of the whales on whose skin flashes of light intermittently revealed tremendous scars. The woman's skin had become quite pliable; she felt neither heat nor cold.

Pieces of net hung from the whales' tails like dead jellyfish around the scars which crisscrossed their bodies. The huge circle was formed by enormous petals; each cetacean's head was at the centre where the wounded whale lay breathing with difficulty. She had been saved from a furious assault probably by killer whales. This is how the mother appeared to Miriam, the whale she had heard so much about and which she had sighted from the lighthouse. Her companions supported her; she was exhausted. She had a scar behind her mouth and a huge slit on her tail, white with parasites.

The other clearly discernible heads swam around, the half-open mouths supportive. They were locked in a carousel which sucked Miriam in. The woman found herself in a blue-bottomed watery enclosure, surrounded by heads. Blue-green eyes stared at her. The whales passed very close to her without touching. The whistling sound in her ear had changed but Miriam was dazed and had ceased listening to it. She let herself slip into the current created by the whales. In the middle, the mother rolled her eyes like disks shining in the sunlight. She had lost her baby. On one side Miriam entered the group swimming, fearful and relaxed. She thought of herself as one of the animals making up the daisy. They were all females except for a young male. Miriam raised her head and saw the cutter not far off, the crew making signals. She did not reply; she did not know what to do. The tone of the clicks and puffs emitted by the whales lowered. She felt she was being brought into an ocean where every act, every impulse rotated around itself, in a different dimension and that the heads of the whales constituted the entrance to this world. How many shipwrecked men had experienced this state? The whales loved the men who swam in the water. They did not attack them, they wished to help, curious about something, a secret that their brain had picked up in the depths. The blue heads around Miriam went under. The mouths disappeared, the changing eyes flashed for an instant, the water streaking them with light. Columns of light shot up and soundlessly disappeared. A mouth opened like a plough churning through the water. They hardly moved, an infinite number of tiny air bubbles trailed behind; only tails burst through the infinity of bubbles on the horizon and disappeared. Miriam turned, bewildered. The daisy was no longer there.

Suddenly the woman was being lifted out of the water. She found herself on a dark island that had unexpectedly appeared. She was frozen with terror, there were no rocks or wrecks in the area. She thought it could be a seaquake.

A gush of steam rose up. Miriam clung to the island, slipping into a niche in the rock like a seaweed torn from the skin of a swimmer. The island bent, displaying its curved profile that shone in the sunset. Everything calmed down and the body of the woman lay almost still. The ground was covered with crustaceans and Miriam compared herself to one of them on a live rock floating in the sea. Or was it the upturned hull of a boat that had come back up to the surface?

She looked towards the cutter which seemed to have stopped, the people on board turned to stone. She waved but no one moved. Miriam was astonished; she was not afraid but rather felt a cold detachment. The whistling sound in her ear had changed; it had become a barely perceptible song. She tried to get to her feet but couldn't. She passed in front of the cutter, outlined against the sun. They all shaded their eyes with their hands so as to see her better. It looked as though they were saluting her. The cutter fell behind; its motor had stopped. Miriam abandoned herself to that strange cavalcade breaking into tears and losing what little strength had remained. She had entered into a fable, or a nightmare, under that splendid sky in the Indian Ocean which was becoming pink as the first stars began to appear. The journey continued as she collapsed, exhausted, her eyes eventually closing in a drowsiness without sleep.

6

The Trincomalee Sea is a blue expanse which in the month of May motionlessly rests on the coral beach. The heat heavily hangs about the tall cliffs. In this season all sorts of cold and warm blooded creatures are washed ashore under the scorching sun, hunter and hunted mingled confusedly together in the tide. The sea sucks a great river into the bay and this mixing of waters brings enormous masses of diatom and plankton which attract squid and whales. In the middle of the bay wander shoals of fish, shellfish, crustaceans, uprooted plants, rusty wrecks, broken-off branches still loaded with fruit. The fishermen cast their nets and gather whatever the sea brings. From these grazing fields of an earthly paradise someone lost at sea may sometimes emerge.

In the late afternoon one day in May a living form was sighted by a fishing boat. A woman who floated with difficulty was pulled out of the water; she breathed easily but was in a confused state of mind. When she was taken to hospital a few abrasions were found on her skin, nothing more. She was about thirty, beautiful, white-skinned. Batticaloa Hospital, where the boat, headed for this southern port, had brought the woman, is a low-set white building surrounded by deep blue fields. The town is a few hundred metres away, suspended in a dense oppressive heat where thin coal-black children play in the streets and herds of fallow deer search for food in the rubbish.

Every day people of all races are admitted to this hospital, cured or sent to the cemetery without too much bother. Only their names and medical data are written down in a great book. For some people not even these details are set down, as in the case of the woman. Medicine here is practiced as a mix of sensitive but informal treatment rich in human sympathy. Illness strikes so frequently in the tropics that it is serenely and fatalistically accepted as part of daily life.

The woman who had come from the sea was put together with other patients in a large room fitted with huge mosquito nets and smelling of lye soap. The shiny red brick floor was marked by the wheels of the skeleton-like painted beds with ornate head-boards. Those intertwining tracks made the room look like a railway station. At the far end a few empty stretchers stood like forgotten carriages. In one corner the beds were piled up with all sorts of equipment. It was the intensive care unit where ceiling fans made the heat a little more bearable. This is where the sun-burnt white-skinned woman lay. She looked like a Shinalese of European descent. She would open her eyes, soundlessly searching for something. There was an absent look about her even though the cardiac readings registered a normal, albeit slightly sluggish, situation.

She woke up twenty-four hours later in a confused state of mind, attempting to emerge from an abyss of broken memories, remains of sensations which evaded her memory. She spoke English with a foreign accent. The doctors could not understand who she was. There was nothing remarkable in this since they were used to similar situations. The woman was identified by the number of her medical file which registered only clinical data. She seemed to have difficulty in hearing. She experienced loneliness and fear although she remembered a strange friendly presence in the water where she had become lost. Her memory returned bit by bit, slowly and with difficulty, among glimmering shapes of uncertain form.

The day after she spoke a few words. The woman in the bed next to her, a Tamil from the north, did not know English, so the first scraps of information were lost. She was moved to another ward for patients with hearing problems.

She slowly recovered but did not seem to hear what was being said to her nor did she seem willing to talk about herself. No one came searching for missing persons. A young Sinhalese woman was placed in the bed next to her and noticed that the woman was recovering. They exchanged a few words, with difficulty, given their respective medical condition, becoming friends in silence. The Sinhalese told her her name, Therese. The other woman couldn't remember hers so Therese called her Marianna. Marianna would listen but did not say much. Then one evening she began to speak in a low voice.

She said that she had to pass on information to a marine research institute: NAS, NAS, she kept repeating. She told of a place in the sea full of fish that spoke like humans and considered the ocean a world in itself.

"You're still all mixed up in the head," said Therese smiling.

"It's a strange place," insisted Marianna. "Maybe the time's not yet ripe for understanding it."

"When will that time come?"

"When we're able to understand its language."

"What language?"

"The language of the air-breathing creatures."

Therese refrained from smiling ironically. She cautiously asked a few more questions but the other woman no longer replied. Therese was a bookbinder, her husband worked for the government. They lived with their three children in a bungalow with wide verandas on the Maduru River. Her hobby was paper painting and she created a sort of little room for herself and Marianna by making partitions with flower-painted cardboard. Here they were able to talk as they wished, interrupted only by the intrusion of the staff. They also dozed frequently.

In the morning they would resume their conversation. Therese often saw beads of perspiration form on the face of her friend, her nostrils quivering and panting. Return to reality was proving difficult. She tried to help Marianna but her attempts to talk were marked by long periods of silence.

"I'd like to go back into the sea," said Marianna one evening, after hours of silence. "I want to finish my research."

"What is it?" asked Therese.

"I'm studying the language of the whales," was the reply. In a faint voice Marianna explained that she was studying the low frequency sounds emitted by the blue whales.

"It's an invisible cord which links them over hundreds of kilometres in the sea."

Therese called a nurse who called a doctor. She told him what she had heard. Although the doctor knew nothing about it, he said that he had heard tales of that sort of experience.

"An invisible cord links them," said Therese. "But there's also another cord that strangles them. The whales live in the midst of these nets. That's what Marianna said."

"How does she know?"

"She's been there, it seems."

"At the bottom of the sea?" said the doctor.

A group of women dressed in loose flapping white clothes came in to tidy up the room, throwing everything around in a gracefully oriental fashion. The conversation was thus interrupted and the doctor went away leaving the two patients in silence, amidst the women who were busily rushing around putting the room in order. Marianna opened her eyes wide, saying something, but no one noticed.

Two days later Therese was discharged. Her husband came to get her, a man with a big belly and a small moustache. Therese whispered something in his ear and he greeted Marianna as though he knew her.

Therese came back to visit Marianna who spoke little and only to her. Then she began to say some names, first that of Felipe so that little by little it was possible to identify the woman.

Marta, Dipika, Luis, the captain and Anthony came, but not Felipe who had gone off on a long voyage. Miriam didn't notice. She asked what had happened in the sea.

They said they had lost sight of her because of the low-set sun and had searched unsuccessfully for hours up and down the coast. The current had dragged Miriam south where the fishing boat picked her up. The boat was working away from its base and the crew had first unloaded the fish, then taken the woman to the port. What Miriam had said at the hospital seemed to be caused by her delirium and no one had considered it important. Things like that happened. The episode was now explained.

Miriam stayed a few more days in hospital and Therese continued her visits as she had also become interested in her friend's story.

"When the whale came up," Miriam told her, "she tried to tell me something. I thought she was a sort of marine mother, attentive in her own way. In any case similar tales are told at NAS, at Colombo . . ."

"Weren't you afraid?"

"It was like a dream."

"How long did it last?"

"I don't know. I didn't have any problems."

"And those lights, those great lights you were always talking about?"

"There were three of them in a triangle, fiery."

"Can't you remember them better?"

"I've been trying to for days. Then I get that sound in my ear and I can't go on. It throws me into confusion."

"Well, let confusion reign, but speak."

"What about? What the whale said?"

"Tell me."

7

The killer whales were biting lips and tail, alternating between the whale and her baby. They especially concentrated on the little one sliding on its mother's belly but they also attacked the mother's lips.

All around the fight had set the waves thrashing in the calm sea as though an island were taking shape in volcanic waters, an island uncertainly rising from the depths with a flock of birds fluttering above.

The mother lifted her head like a lever, flinging a white-toothed assailant from her lips. With her tail she lashed out at two others, flinging them into the air and setting free the calf who was being attacked. Taking in air for the deep dive that would save her, she went down waiting for the baby to follow but it didn't. The whale came back up, her tail whirling, and shielded the baby who was losing blood as the killer whales resumed the attack. Under the bright sun the whale resumed her fight, taking in air. The baby was trembling and squealing. It was her weak point: she had to defend it, make it breathe, drag it down in the deep dive where the killers could not follow. But it was wounded, frightened, and under attack by the dogs of the sea, everyone's enemy. The mother shaped her nostrils into a short proboscis which expelled a column of steam. The parasitic crustaceans hung on to her skin even more tightly. Every other creature had disappeared, even the pilot fish that take advantage when the great whales go past.

The surviving killer whales spread out in order to concentrate their attack on the smaller prey that the mother defended with such devastating blows. Then they charged. Their mouths open, ready to bite, emitted an unexpected mosquito-like sound. Their bites cut like razors and had marked the skins and tails of whales that had been killed or had survived. They would feast later.

The whale struck the first assailant with her tail, severing its head. The others followed and the blue giant spun over, hitting them sideways so as to shield the little one swimming alongside. The whale and her calf needed to inhale great quantities of air, dissolve it quickly in the blood and dive down hundreds of metres. But the fight used up oxygen. The blue water became tinged with red; in the middle of it all the baby was trembling in a violet haze.

Under the equatorial sun the water formed ever-changing prisms. The struggling bodies were a confusion of spheres; the killer whales, evil balls that had to be crushed with the tail. They would dissipate, then return with renewed fury. The whale had become a spring loaded with hate – the only type of hate she knew – defending her child. Increasingly red, violet, black, the baby floundered in the grip of the white jaws of the killer whales that were biting it. The black became violet, indigo, blue. Then it all disappeared.

Now the enormous whale was alone. Five or six killer whales were biting her sides, her fins. From the front a blue whirlwind bore down on the attackers, sweeping them away. It enclosed the whale in a convolvulus circle.

The other whales had come, forming a defensive ring around their exhausted companion who had lost her child.

On the outside the killer whales spun in a tired carousel as they retreated under the attack of the newly arrived giants. Fear is a rare emotion for them and is expressed by a bloodless squealing. Further away, a blood-soaked baby whale reduced to a trunk had become the centre of a furious swirl, a vortex formed by all sorts of predators where the killer whales had to contend with fish and birds. The dogs of the sea had been followed by the jackals. The orgy merged into the horizon. The other circle remained, glimmering on the flat ocean in front of the white-green coast where a lighthouse pointed sharply towards the sky. The whales formed a tight circle around their wounded companion, gusts of steam coming out of the short proboscis on top of their head. Their faces were like flat rostra with blue-green eyes set on the ends.

The mother washed her wounds with wide-ranging movements. The bites had created new furrows on her tail. She now swam in the midst of the group of friends who had come to her aid.

The memory of the attack, the death of the baby, descended within her. The killer whales had attacked in a pack but now the roles had been reversed and the predators had fled. The fight had ended but her child was lost.

Dusk descended, sparse clouds reflected in the water.

In the clear air and the dazzling light of the setting sun the whales saw a row of oblong bouncing forms drawing away.

One of those dry whales incapable of submersion had arrived from the horizon and clinging to it were the giant sea-horses of the land who so often lay in wait for the whales.

The dry whale lowered its strange ears into the sea to listen under water. On top huge white fins spread out; the parasites, those vertical creatures similar to giant sea-horses, moved around them. The ears descended to the bottom, thread-like and hard as the tentacles of the octopus. This is how the sea-horses of the land listened. This strange whale was different from those of the sea; it always went home with its parasites – they too were unable to descend into the depths.

One of the females turned to the mother, exchanging signals expressed by means of certain sounds. The sea-horse's ears recorded:

"Mrr, mnniiem, I miss him, rarfurr, raar."

"Pfrrm, piffr, piffer."

"Mrr, Mnniem."

Then the daisy formation went down. The oval petals sank keeping the little ones in the middle. Only the central stamen remained: the mother.

8

The great creature swam alone, upwards and downwards strokes balanced by the fins, little wings on an immense body. The call came again but from another source. It jolted the female. Something was calling her, exciting her, like a spasm in her belly, awakening her instinct. The ocean was a territory suited to the hugeness of the creature; blood and fat helped her to penetrate it from the icy wastes of the Antarctic to the warm waters of the equator.

The blue whales had lived in this element for millions of years, without protective lairs, feeding and fasting in alternate seasons.

Their only enemies were the dogs of the sea, the killer

whales. A few generations ago another enemy had appeared: those big sea-horses of the land, their eyes ready to strike swiftly. They travelled over the seas, stuck like parasites on the backs of huge shells similar to empty whales. In the last few seasons they had wreaked tremendous slaughter among the whales with a fiery sting. The surviving whales would call out to each other from the bottom of the sea, separated by ever increasing distances. But the females, with their remarkable sense of solidarity, sometimes attempted to direct a song-like call to the sea-horses of the land too. Their dream was to achieve a song of solidarity linking the whole planet.

The huge female continued to swim towards the open sea. She danced as she replied to the call, searching out in her organs the whistling sounds used by the species. She felt empty and, matching her call to the echo of the still persistant sound she had heard, she transmitted again. Miles away an adult male was racing through the waves. He came from the cold seas, brought here by his instinct: the time for love had come.

The call of the female unrolled, enveloped him. The male, a deep blue bull, leapt out of the waves meeting the air with deep bellowing sounds. Other males heard him and, uncertain, left the way open for him. Others gave chase but he outdistanced them all. They gave up uncaring since they could feel the strength in the vibrations he emitted. The mating season had begun.

The female continued to transmit her call, sounds made up of detached consonants and rolling notes.

"Mrr, miiraaa, mmn, mm, rr, ar, arr . . ."

Her cry travelled over the waters. Then came the silence that transformed it into an unknown language. It reached the bottom of the female's brain, registered, and was thus perceived.

"Mira, mirr . . ."

The female turned towards the call.

"Mia, mrr, mi, mia, faa, aaarr . . ."

The reply was immediate. Come, it kept whispering, come. The call vibrated on the ocean floor, pulsated among the other languages in that opaque wateriness, through channels opened in the depths. It throbbed, condensed: "Mmoe, mira, rraah, mm, son, accan mi ap . . ."

The crustaceans and shellfish clinging to their huge muzzles were crushed and swept away in the blue waters, as the two creatures met, coupled, embraced, slid dancing one on top of the other to the rhythm of the song the female kept softly humming.

They raced for a few miles, under the sparkling sky, overtaking shoals of dolphins and tuna that dissolved like every other image in the passing of the two great beasts.

The white-green coast remained in sight. Along the coast the empty whale that carried those strange seahorses of the land emitted harsh banging sounds.

The female pushed forward turning towards the male, her mouth slightly open, sliding along his side.

Spinning, they went down and came up again in a turmoil of water. The mouth of the male marked the skin of his companion; the skin folded inwards, in her dilated eyes, clear in the amber light of the surface. The couple rolled on the boundaries of the water; they made love, the warm sea as their bed, in front of the huge bay under the hills. The rhythmic movement of the male sent the female under water. Using his tail he positioned himself on top, his fins taking hold of her striped belly while his organ snaked out. Clashes and caresses were replaced by a vibration, *mira, mirr, aaar,* a low tonality which slowly rose upwards. In the warm waters of the ocean the union common to all animals, which explodes when life decides to reproduce, was being re-enacted.

The male bore down on his companion warming to her with a push which the water supported.

A shoal of crest-backed tuna passed by. Some jellyfish with bush-like tentacles unfolded, yellow as the morning sun. The sea became turquoise.

Tails began to move in a twisting pattern, uniting and separating. They beat one against the other in the throes of orgasm, then came to rest, pointing towards the sky, soft under the light of the sun. Afterwards they sank in the dusk, into the sea pulsating with life. The two animals separated; the male swiftly disappeared, while the female took on an indigo hue. A giant squid blotted out every other form. The heart of the mother quickened its beat as she dived into the depths where few lights shone upwards through the dark. In the distance a larger three-pointed flame burned brightly. As the pressure increased the blood of the whale, saturated with oxygen, rushed quickly and impetuously. In her dive the cetacean dragged down a bundle of torn seaweed; the crushed remains of the crustaceans clung to her muzzle. Each element was adapted to the depths. The mother's head pointed downwards, the only warm-blooded being to descend so deep. Far away on other routes, other females, now mothers, were undertaking the same journey. At the bottom of the sea they would concentrate the instinct of life fusing it within themselves, beside a fire which was burning under the canopy of the night.

9

The vision of the depths was revealed at two hundred metres. All vegetation had disappeared. On the ocean floor three craters appeared on the scene. Now the whale was alone. She dived further down. In her belly unidentified lumps fused with the oxygen in her blood.

Her tail bored through the sea. Below, the mouths of the craters gave out a warm glow, weakly lighting those underwater hills. The mother reached the bottom with its sand and mud banks rich in diatoms, where a new contingent of crustaceans and shellfish awaited her. With her fins the cetacean dug into that dark larder, absorbing dense food which the difference in pressure would help to dissolve into her body. In that maternal fibre pressed in the depths, the act of love consummated on the surface, under the sun, was undergoing its evolution.

The mothers came down that area delineated by the three volcanos, instinctively keeping an obscure appointment. They were subject to a trial set since time immemorial, their organism compressed by the pressure almost as though to test their powerful structure, their glands transmitting a particular type of message.

The whale's movements became progressively slower, as if in a temple where each gesture has an air of gravity about it. Entering the area in the middle of the craters, she swam forward with forced strokes, heart crushed by the pressure, and headed for the middle of the luminous source, searching for heat rather than light. She swam until the pressure forced her to keep a horizontal plane, to open her mouth slightly filling it with dense, nourishing water. Her eyes rotated in order to observe the ocean floor.

The floor was a rocky crust spread with pearly lava which refracted the viscosity of the craters. Animals of stratified form moved in the absence of vegetation, their carnivorous nature causing them to devour each other. The plain petered out in formless agglomerations marked by pinnacles and rocky outcrops.

Dragging her jaw, the whale uprooted formless

lumps of matter that discharged a cloud of shellfish and crustaceans which vied with each other in their attempts to assail her. The hoeing continued in the sand and the mud, the cetacean hovering above the ocean floor like a dark bird. In front of her, like a prehistoric battleship, a nautilus swam with two serpentine annelids in a death grip. The three animals separated, disappearing in the blackness when they were hit by the whale.

The whale headed for an indistinct muddle of chela and a tangle of loricates. In that darkness, agressiveness was expressed through a distant dance.

The great warm-blooded animal stopped. Only the males of another type of cetacean, the sperm-whale, went further into the deep. One of them was there, in front of the blue whale.

Its square head was thrusting its jaw towards a giant squid whose tentacles were tearing at its skin. The squid was gripping the cetacean in an attempt to immobilise its jaw as the two bodies twisted and turned in a terminal dance. The pressure made the sperm-whale move slowly as it attacked the darting tentacles of its mortal enemy.

The battle continued, illuminated by the nearby crater. The whale kept tearing at the squid which seemed to empty itself in order to resist. The whale became aware of a second obstacle, a transparent treacherous tentacle he had been dragging around for some time: it was a piece of net that had wrapped itself around him, one of those thrown into the water by the seahorses of the land.

As the whale passed, the area was covered with muddy dust, splattered with ink and blood. The blows of the two combatants tore the ground open, uncovering for an instant millions of tiny animals who quickly scuttled back into hiding. A phosphorescent fish traced a luminous line between the blue whale and the two adversaries. The battle ended and the whale swam away squeezing more oxygen from its muscles. Her womb palpitated, a whistling sound invaded her ears, her blood quickened its flow and rushed to an obscure lake in the inner reaches of her body, gushing into a cavity compressed by the pressure. In that instant the whale felt her maternity, a sensual pain, then just pain, a more vital impulse than the survival instinct.

She swam with difficulty, heading for an appointment in the crater area where no living being could bear the heat but where, at the edges, teemed an infinite number of micro-organisms like beggars at the palace gates.

On the slopes of a glassy crater there was a sunken artefact, an old high-sterned ship, its deck all broken up. Behind it the light outlined a vivid and at the same time arid picture. The mother penetrated this zone, hovering between the crater and the wreck. She was enveloped by a hot mist that crushed her. Her jaw and throat gave way, widening disjointedly. Her mouth turned into the mouth of a reptile, then of a frog and finally of a fish of the depths, tremendously wide. Her backbone was deformed by the pressure and rebounded resiliently. Violent jolts twisted her skeleton but the whale withstood them, altering her profile. She dilated her rib cage as her muscles tensed like steel springs. Under the skin, tail and fins became thread-like. The mother took on the shape of an octopus; she expanded like an amoeba in oval shapes, all the while enveloped in the hot mist. Liver and heart were crushed, kidneys disintegrated like slush. She continued to swim towards the source of the heat. A chain of giant salpa surrounded her as the mist caused by the suspension from the ocean floor punctuated the view. In the lobes of the cranium, the brain was flattened and sensations became indistinct, uniting the various organs in a fluid experience. The salpa disappeared. A cetacean with deformed muzzle and frayed teeth continued its slow advance followed by a second and then by a third ghost-like form. On the ocean floor the volcano lashed out a tongue of fire which outlined the whale in diaphanous strips and a luminous halo.

The mother forced her pace, gently moving the fringes of skin that seemed to have formed at her extremities with a gentle wing-like motion, stretching in length as she swam. She had returned to a forgotten age. It became increasingly difficult for her to go forward, so she stopped, letting herself drift with the current. Her profile blended with that of a lamellate organism, a serpentine form that enveloped her. They were both dragged along by a horizontal whirlpool. An unidentifiable source gave them strength: energy penetrated skin, heart, kidneys, even the compressed muscles. The two intertwined animals were attacked by a swarm of green shellfish that had emerged from the hot mist. The shellfish attacked, boring through the surface layers of their skins with astonishing results: the organisms formed a single pulsating being which exuded a rapidly spreading oily substance. It went up, came down again, heavily breaking through watery outcrops, a violent primordial force that swept away every living thing in the vicinity and thrust forward, rampant, like a formless creature: a leviathan. The shellfish continued their attack on skin and lips of the cetacean, still intertwined with the lamellate organism until they separated, struck by a sudden discharge.

The mother emerged deprived of identity. She hovered over the ocean floor, out of control, without a sense of direction. Nothing and everything belonged to her as she pulsated, rolling. She continued her dance alone, transforming her body into that of a Bacchante, drinking a wine-coloured sea. Her tail beat the glassy mud, raising twisted figures in unusual shapes.

She rolled towards the crater she had almost reached, its luminescent edge traversed by a column of clear water.

She quivered under the jet of water, letting herself go belly side up, feeling it pulse through her body. All warm-blooded creatures belonged to her, all creatures formed inside her or turned to her for support with subtle stimulus. She felt a tightening in her nipples.

The pulsing motion changed. The green mist dissolved in an eddy, a detonation that increased the flexibility of the enormous pressure. She felt a desire, an all-eveloping dissipation which dispersed the pulse in swirls right to the tail. She was becoming a mother again; it always happened when she returned down here, after the act of love. She advanced into the hot water that surrounded the craters. They were small, perfect in form and erupted a glassy material that solidified immediately, forming deposits on the slopes and refracting light into the clear water. The craters had always been a stable feature of that landscape. No life form ever came within one or two miles in that sea of decomposed sulphides and salts. Lava scoriae flowed down the craters' slopes together with rolling stones to form a lifeless rock garden. Only the mother, the strongest living creature of all, crossed it. She overcame barriers of heat and cold, dancing to a majestic rhythm. Her eyes were fixed on the nearest crater which looked like a burning eye following that strange apparition as the two faced each other in close encounter, separated only by a layer of spring water.

The mother stared at the incandescent eye until the glare blinded her momentarily. Then the vision changed and the sea revealed one of its mysteries of origin.

The mother was passing through the darkness filled with other organisms deprived of strength. The rapid effusion and its inversion marked the dance of the animals, and the whale was an extreme example.

The cetacean transmitted her call which was received where the lines of air and water meet, on the calm sea where one of those strange seahorses of the land was swimming.

Time on the surface was different, stimuli were less inhibited. The whale's call surfaced, was picked up by the floating body and the pulse of the mother was projected into the human.

The whale had reached the limit of resistance. She headed for air, supported by an upward current. She gave up her body to the water and was lifted up by similar forms that had appeared around her.

The eyes of the cetacean were blinded by the glare of the sun. The mother dilated her blowholes with a puff that immediately dispersed in the heat of the day as the air rushed in through the same apertures, tumultuously flooding the exhausted lungs an instant later.

10

The whale had now come back, blowing in the sunlight in Trincomalee Bay.

Approaching the coast she observed it as if it were a lost horizon, rendered restricting by her migrations, arid by her habits, crowded with little creatures among which the big sea-horse whose real kingdom lay there.

The mother gave birth near the borders of that kingdom, warm water bays far from rip tides and killer whales where the babies could learn the ways of the sea without being exposed to danger. But it was always necessary to be on the alert; the sea-horses of the land were dangerous. The whale decided to turn back; she was afraid now. Better the high seas where dangers were predictable and the expanses for diving limitless.

The mother swam down the shelf as the water pressed in on her, heart beating harder and dissolving the oxygen. The compression revitalized her organs, all the way to the brain where memory and instinct flowed together.

The mother rolled over and plugged into a flow of messages which came from far away. They told about a storm at sea and one of their kind in need of help on a beach to the east.

The call came from a male stranded on a faraway shore. It saw the beach as an open shell that sucked the water away from his back, scalding it. The movement of the undertow awakened lost memories, fusing fear and nostalgia.

The cetacean was observing the sea-horses of the land on the shore. They were waiting. Violent splashes showed the attempts made by the animal to free itself while its closed mouth transmitted the call for help. Three female whales had picked it up and were converging on the stranded animal, following its call, a very low-pitched wail that jolted the receptive system of the species, ploughing through the waves like a cry of anguish. Then one of the females received another, more kindred, call and gave up the race, taking a path through underwater gorges in a strait bristling with submerged mountains. The other two continued their journey and as the male heard them approach he tried to turn in the water which covered only half its body.

From the shore the sea-horses of the land began uttering deadened sounds, transmitting signals to each other. Five of them entered the water and approached the male who heard their incessant gurgling but was not frightened; he still wanted to cross beyond the limits of the water, propelled by that strange nostalgia that had pushed it towards the land.

There, rocks and boulders had broken up and the water, evaporated for ever, only fell as rain. Dryness dominated, a feeling of death for a cetacean. The sea-horses of the land had overcome that feeling; their skin breathed parched air.

The whales instead needed a coating of water, thinner or thicker according to the depth, that allowed them to go everywhere without suffering heat or cold.

On the beach of that scorching island, two species faced each other.

The sea-horses of the land wanted to seize the cetacean or throw it back into the sea; it was too large to remain there. It, instead, felt an attraction to the land that over-rode all precaution, yet cried out to its nearby companions for help to be freed from the trap which held it fast. The mother and the other female arrived.

When they saw the three cetaceans together, the sea-horses of the land that had entered the sea backed out of the water and sat down, waiting. A few hours passed but nothing happened, as the females kept trying to push their stranded companion back into the water. During these attempts, between waves and undertow, one of the females was beached too but managed to free itself by twisting and turning, and flapping its tail, leaving a furrow and a dune on the sand. The two females renewed their efforts to move their companion.

The male had been lured into approaching the shore in the hope of satisfying an obscure instinct that led to ancient paths lost in the process of evolution. Now it communicated its disappointment with its shallow breathing as the females continued their attempts amidst the covering waves, slipping and sliding like the wheels of a bogged vehicle.

A crystal sun shone in the sky above; in the background, against its light, the sea-horses of the land watched, standing in a row near a herd of empty whales that had been pulled to shore.

The mother opened her mouth, directing a torrent of spray onto the back of the male who was suffering from the heat of the sun.

Together they pushed their heads in the shallow water and lay still, as though dead. They communicated with low deep sounds.

"Marra, mmm, arra, mar, marr, mrmrrr . . ."

"Uur, buur, rr, uiur, tur, reee, fuur . . ."

"Mmar, miaar, marr, orrrn, orr, or, or . . ."

The acoustic recordings analysed the messages as composed of five consonants and an equal number of vowels, forming a conversation that evoked instinctive sensations at the same time. Translated, it could perhaps have meant:

"Let's return to the blue pastures, marr . . ."

"Help me, help . . ."

The reception scrambled becoming a scale of disconnected sounds. An hour passed, then the male gave up completely, its motionless body half immersed in the water; its eyes had lost their shine and had become glassy. The two females retreated towards the open sea, listening to the feeble calls of the companion they were leaving, continuing to transmit whispers and vibrations. Then the eves lost the reflection of the volcano. As they regained the open sea, a calf approached them and began to bump against one of the females. It had been waiting for them.

Their tails propelled them towards the ocean. Back on the beach, a few hundred metres away, a whale had just died.

11

The two females swam on in the dark with the little one. The pressure pushed into their skins and their bodies responded, rapidly adapting. The mother kept transmitting location signals to her companion. A third female appeared, attracted by the wide-ranging vibrations. They had reached the blue country of the whales. A fourth female joined the group. They swam down through the water in a spiral, in a sort of convolvulus pattern that transmitted charges of energy. Each one formed part of a whole as the ocean floor came up to meet them, like a dark plant opening out in the dim light under increasing pressure that altered gravity, developing into strange forms. The little one and its mother left the group and swam to the surface, while the others continued their dive into the depths.

They danced forming a pattern that lost animal nature and acquired a flowery consistency, each one turned towards its companions, tails pointing out.

Around them all stood still. The mother extended her fins, and this was the stamen in the flower she was forming with the others. Her companions imitated her. All feeling of hostility and solitude ceased. The huge petals were shaken by the sound of a far-away eruption. Horizons widened, as other, disconnected, vibrations arose in the darkness.

Chains of bodies and of humours became alive in the dance. The current created by their rotation became a whirlpool. Flowers blossomed generating curved buds; the compact ones managed to survive while the others disintegrated. The turbulence raised by the whales shook the ocean floor as the cetaceans came closer together and the strange flower opened out, no longer individuals but simply life. The weight of the sea dragged the unusual form back to a remote past.

The oxygen supply almost exhausted in lungs and muscles, the cetaceans began to surface, one after the other. The flower took on a violet hue, then blue, as it released a wave of solidarity. Even when far away from each other, they would no longer be separated. The vertebrae of the mother stretched as she rose towards the surface, flying high.

The flower began to shed its petals as the animals retreated one at a time, breaking up the corolla. On the surface the circle would be formed again to assist one of their kind in trouble or to help other groups of females and their little ones.

For millions of years the blue whales, queens of the depths, had blown these feelings towards the sky, communicating in their own fashion the secret that had made them great and peaceful. Sometimes they would approach the shore to do this but someone would run aground and the others would go back to the sea. On the land life was inflexible; in the sea it was different. The brain of the mother pulsed with these feelings; it had only a faint idea of life on dry land. She had seen a few clumsy tapirs come out of the forest; animals without a hint of harmony about them. On the land a carnivorous intelligence reigned; the whale had occasionally observed the meat eaters.

The cetacean surfaced, reappearing in the clear ocean. Her brain underwent decompression and the mother woke up completely. Floating slowly over the ripples caused by her emergence, she blew a jet of vapour that vanished into the sky. She collided with a wave. Her kingdom was down there even if her lungs breathed up here, on the surface; everything else, including her brain, functioned under water. She was the largest living creature, the queen of the sea, but she had to come out of it in order to breathe.

The whale rolled away from the spot where she had emerged. She could hold her breath for ten, twenty minutes, even longer, then blow a jet of air several metres into the air. She blew towards the sky. Within she felt tranquillity return, still followed by the dark. If she had returned to travel over earthly shores and rivers, perhaps the blue of her skin would have turned into something less pliable, taking on another colour where everything disappears and recommences, nobody knows how. Many beings on the planet had already gone through this experience.

She looked towards the land. The band of green overrun by the blue sky was enticing. The whale could barely make out colours, but she was attracted by sounds. Perhaps in one of the land creatures were the remnants of another age when colours and sounds shone together: sea-horses and whales. Perhaps this was the secret. However, that this should happen on dry land was strange, not at all instinctive. There, everything lacked fluidity, whereas the sea allowed its denizens complete freedom of movement, right to the bottom of the deep. That was the place, the heart of existence. The intertwined daisy formation of the whales showed the blooming of a lasting harmony better than any other form of expression. This had to be communicated to the more evolved species; it had to be communicated in order to widen the links. Perhaps only then would the daisies be able to dance on this planet.

She dived again, going down deep. The pressure pressed in on her; the phenomena of the deep returned once more. Then she turned towards the light and swam upwards. The change in pressure caused an upheaval in her brain; one part continued to live the experience of the great deep, the other kept rising with the body. It was a trait of the cetaceans that led to the distortion of reality as if sleep and vigil, memory and instinct, coexisted. The mother entered a particular band of blue which helped the hemispheres of the brain get back into synch; the whale's body was about to surface, but part of her brain continued dreaming.

12

She moved her fins slowly as she swam in the calm sea. A series of pulses propelled her into a world better known to man through images than through sounds. For the whale, sound was music she took with her, lightly wrapped in some vision or other. She was accompanied by another whale who swam beside her, sending out signals every so often. The sheltering ocean was all around them.

The mother was dreaming of her world, the sea. It was like a sort of electric arc that ran through her brain.

Dreaming, she descended to the depths where plankton is replaced by deep sea benchtos, like a prickling mist around phosphorescent organisms. Fear increases if the oxygen supply runs low in these circumstances, and sometimes the brain, highly stressed, flees to the past as though in search of a maternal nest of reassuring memories.

The whale swimming beside her entered into her dream and the communication between the two creatures increased in intensity, each one instilling in the other a part of herself, while their sensitive hearing did the rest. A syntonic world was created in which the whales danced singing and their melody spread throughout the depths. Other cetaceans joined in, creating a prayer of the wilds – *bee mat, beem, mammaat* – as time rolled backwards, ever backwards.

A dot of reddish-beaked birds with pointed wings was flying over the sea. The wind puffed up their feathers, pushing them towards the land into a tangle of spiky trees.

Down in the sea a sluggish mammal floated in the lee of a volcanic island.

It was an afternoon millions of years ago. The sun had passed its zenith and was descending towards the west in the hot air. From the trees, populated by an unusual-looking fauna, a group of squirrels finished devouring an enormous quantity of succulent stone-fruit, dripping thick oily juice. They then bounded down to the rose-coloured beach, forming wide circles at the lagoon, where the line of surf marks the boundary of the sea. In front of them floated a huge beast as blue as the sky. The black eyes of the rodents were fixed on its enormous body drifting in the weak current. Its ears, little slits in the head with highly sensitive receptive capacity, revealed what was happening in front, on the shore. The squirrels were now following a calcareous water stream that flowed silently down to the sea.

When they reached the shore the rodents began to smell out molluscs and shells. Tense and afraid, they scurried up and down along the water line, ears and whiskers pricked up. Every so often, they would run round in a circle, one behind the other, to replace fear with courage. In front of them a stationary whale was blowing.

Its auricular fissures, open so wide that they hurt, gathered in every sound within range. It followed the squirrels, the sound made by their paws, the squeals uttered as they sucked molluscs. In the water the yellow sand on the bottom was lit up by flashes of silvery fish in flight. An otter with a huge tail and webbed paws appeared on the land and the squirrels backed away rapidly, except for a little one who remained in the clutches of the tawny-skinned aggressor covered by pearly beads of water that shone like pearls. The parents attacked the predator's muzzle, causing it to lose its balance and fall squealing violently. But it did not let go of its prey. The whale watched.

The struggling animals were being violently shaken by something it knew; it was a convulsive vibration. The otter attacked the two squirrels who had scratched its muzzle. The whale's slitted ears picked up the call of death.

Half submerged in the water, the otter ran along the borders of its world. Otter and squirrels slipped and rolled towards the shore. Long ago the cetaceans too had had their beginnings on the land but they had fled from it to wander in the vast expanse of the sea. Sometimes they met the otters in the sea, animals undecided whether to live on the land or in the water. This meant an ability to take risks, and intelligence. But was a high degree of intelligence really necessary? And was it really a mark of intelligence to need so many changes? That was what the whale thought about it. It fed at certain times and could go months without eating, just as it could go for an hour without breathing. Its needs were very modest, this was the special quality that created its ability to give, to offer. Otters and squirrels also had this ability, but mainly during the mating season and only for their mate, for their little ones. They had never known social maternity, a feeling possessed only by the great cetaceans. The otter bit its small prey which remained lifeless in its mouth, while the two parents fled, powerless.

The whale attempted to go up the beach but got stuck. Even in that environment it did not feel it had any enemies, it was only incapable of movement. It tried to understand the sounds coming from the land. Who was master there? A giant animal?

The otter swam towards the whale. As it drew near, the cetacean was able to see it rather than hear it and the two animals observed each other.

The otter had a very small head, the other animal an enormous one. Both puffed; an exchange of air between sky and body. The otter, frightened yet attracted, began to swim around the whale, sniffing the giant's sides. It was a pervasive scent with a sense of immensity which disoriented the otter, used as it was to hide and hunt in restricted tracts of water.

The giant it was sniffing at came from the sea. It was an astounding being, beyond the otter's reach or ken. The otter had seen something similar, just as big, on the land; a tapir-like animal that had emerged from the river by the sea. It was as huge as the whale, perhaps even larger, and the otter's predatory instincts were obliterated by its size. The huge tapir took no notice of the otter; wherever it walked all other creatures scuttled away. It dominated the land. The otter experienced the same feeling in front of the whale; it was entering a luminous cavern, half filled with water, where the predatory instinct, so essential to its survival, underwent a change. What lay beyond that blue threshold?

The two creatures confronted each other, their heads half out of the water; each felt an obscure impulse which their throats were not able to transform into sound.

The otter flipped over on its side, pouncing on a fish and quickly gobbled it down. Its stomach full, it went back to the shore as the waves broke nearby. The atmosphere had become tense. Rivulets snaked into swamps which were indistinguishable from the sea in that sultry climate in a scenario dominated by a smouldering volcano that looked about to erupt. The nostrils of the mother were pointed towards its hot breath, as were the nostrils of others of her kind who were approaching the shore from the deep. The nostrils protruded forward, forming an arch on the shrunken muzzle. Proportions became inverted and the cetaceans observed from the froth of the waves the place where, on the shore, ran the otter who had grown huge out of all proportion. The animal stopped, directing its gaze towards the sea where other whales floated. The wind shook leaves and sounds, mixing strong smells to that of sulphur.

The birds with the long pointed wings and the saw-toothed rostrum flew across the sky again uttering hoarse cries. The whales listened as they rested on the shallow ocean bed. Their ears, buried in the masses of fat that separate the skin from the internal organs, received staccato cries, sounds travelling more across time than across space. Low tide crashed on the beach. The otter, silhouetted against the light, grew larger, turning into a wolf with tremendous jaws. Time rolled on. Millennia rushed by.

The great wolf rushed at the crabs that had changed colour and shone under a new sun. Their white stringy meat squelched out of the shells. Then the wolf gobbled the empty shells too as the waves washing on the shore matted its fur with golden plankton. The two cetaceans in the sea now had a small muzzle, like that of a crocodile, and short stumpy legs that helped them move about in the water. The wolf jumped on the smaller of the two, springing back to land after its useless attack. The wolf and the sea beasts had something in common, something warm between the palpitations in the stomach. The blue-eyed wolf stared motionless; only a slight crumpling of the fur, which moved up and down, showed its jaws to the animals in the sea. Under the line of the forest that enveloped the red volcano, a herd of horses of Lilliputian proportions were neighing in the sun. They stood smaller than the wolf and pawed the ground with the crown of their hooves, trembling because they were so tiny compared to their enormous enemy. The wolf, who had paws like those of a bear, continued its splashing run along the water line. Up in the sky the clouds stood still.

The wolf looked round for a companion who had remained some distance away so that they could attack the horses before they were swallowed up by the forest with the rose-coloured leaves. A blood-red colour began to spread over both plants and animals as the wolf went on running.

The cetaceans followed the scene from the water. Splendid insects traced sinusoidal patterns as they flew through the air to attack the little horses who shooed them away by swinging their tails without taking their eyes off the running predator. Now it looked less like a wolf and more like an otter. The whales picked up every sound made by the creatures on the land, identifying cries of hunger and of fear. Before them the animals moved in concentric circles.

Everyone was hunting for something: clumps of grass or other animals. The otter had sprung, cutting an oblique path between the horses and the bush as the little quadrupeds rushed galloping into the forest, disappearing into the rose-coloured foliage amid squeals and the sound of galloping hooves. A ghostly creature covered with spiky scales, hanging from the branch of a bottle-shaped tree, rolled its eyes, firey in the shade and grey in the light. It gave out a blood-curdling cry as it jumped to the ground in an upright position, as the sea-horse does in the water to free itself from entangling seaweed. The cetaceans concentrated their attention on this noise which was followed by another, louder one. Enormous tapirs came out of the backdrop of rose-coloured leaves that enveloped the forest. It opened up and the trees were hit by a violent wind that set the tapirs fleeing amid high-pitched trumpeting sounds. The bark of the otter and the neighing of the little horses were heard again.

On the shore the biped ghost-like creature was whistling. It jumped on the beach uttering a strange sort of cry. It supported itself on only two limbs. Uttering a whistle like the cry of a new-born baby, it approached a small rodent who, crazed with fear, attacked it. Behind it, another biped was communicating with its companion transmitting a strange sort of silent whistling sound that was perceived even by the whales. In the sky above the wind was gathering masses of clouds.

Half submerged in the lagoon, the cetaceans continued to listen. In their dilated eyes the scenario kept disappearing and reappearing.

Time marched on for millions of years. The landscape widened and narrowed, at times covered by the waves, the same again after an infinite number of days. Now the sun was warm and the sea had retreated. The cetaceans were still there. They gravitated towards the bottom of the lagoon attracted by the sounds and by the whistle of the ghost-like animal who was still there silently watching the whales. It was the meeting of two different species which for some mysterious reason were attracted to each other. The sea-horse of the land emitted a whistle, then a repetitive modulated shout that entered the ear of the whale creating an intense unknown impression. Above, the flight of sharp-winged birds again crossed the sky, their beaks open in a cry among swarms of horrendous insects. On the calm sea, the light of the setting sun tinged the cliffs beyond the shore where the forest dropped in a blood-red colour. There the big sea-horse of the land was chasing a shrew mouse. The two figures locked, then separated with fluid movements. The leaves of the coconut trees on the shore brought the whispers of the land to the cetaceans and stimulated their desire to slither in the dry. Their uneasiness grew until, all together, they slid backwards into the water.

Periods of waking and dreaming continued to alternate as the whales, crushed by the pressure, descended again into the depths. This caused the distortion of memory, together with the deformation of the head and the body crushed by a storm deep down.

13

Waking and dreaming had become separate; the brain regained its normal function, the head resumed its normal shape. It brought back to the whale's consciousness behaviour patterns that the ocean floor had reawakened. The whale felt alive, anxious to communicate its impetuous outburst. It swam through the blue water heading for the surface.

The sea was the same colour as the whale which was only visible because of the myriad of small organisms that surrounded it. Fish and silvery molluscs moved like little points of light in a stellar system that was the colour of the sky. It was a blind planetarium. Parallel to it there was an acoustic one that the whale was traversing. Each fish left a trial of sound in its wake and the mother chose the most silent, least crowded, route. She continued to go up in search of air. The degree of her sensitivity changed with the change in pressure.

The mother became aware of the change in her blood. The ocean floor rushed away, becoming a distant static entity. Down there the mountains and volcanos were strong, masculine. They poured heat on the bodies of the females when they descended, charging them with energy and emptying them of individuality. The whale increased the propulsive force of her tail; she was on her way back to the surface.

As the dark receded, becoming an echo of the past, the brain put away memories of past ages.

The mother did not possess vocal chords and her stormy memory pressed in on her. Her tissues had undergone regeneration on the ocean floor, where nothing changed, except through volcanic activity.

That was where life began, primitive forms condensing into beings of enormous size that the buzzing of the depths revealed obscure primeval matrices. The blue whale increased her speed, crossing a shoal of tuna and ramming a killer whale that was approaching her. She had forgotten the intensity of the depths, regaining her agility as the pressure eased. A rhythmic sensation had entered her body. Her fins stretched to the greatest possible width and her eyes opened like a grapnel that hooked onto reality. She had never met a creature like her in size, nor had she felt in any other creature a similar serenity. Her muscles squeezed the last available oxygen from the myoglobin. Her eyes saw one of the false whales that transported the sea-horses of the land. She avoided a group of sting-rays that were following the same route and ran into a river of yellowish plankton as thick as a fog. She swam through shoals of crustaceans, her favourite food during the cold season, but her lips remained closed. She had lost her child, put to death by the killer whales, but the need to give recurred with spasmodic insistence. It had already happened: the encounter with the male and the descent to the volcanos had initiated a new cycle. Her dilated eyes gathered unusual images: squirting turbot and ink-fringed squid. A sea-horse of the land was floating on the surface. The mother noticed that it communicated over great distances like the whales.

The sea-horses of the land invaded the sea more frequently than they used to. Perhaps they wanted to communicate with the whales but in that case they had to listen too.

Now the mother was observing one of them floating in the sea where they usually only came riding on the empty whales. Perhaps there was some way of communicating.

Sometimes a cetacean rushing towards a beach had tried it but then it had run aground on the sand.

The sea-horse of the land swam awkwardly. It was a female and the females of certain species often had the impulse to communicate and to help. Perhaps that was the case with her.

The whale blew then silently filled her lungs. The sea-horse had come close and the mother headed towards her swimming over a coral garden. On the other side of that boundary lived the sea-horses of the land. They suckled their babies and looked after them for years, like the whales. The more they loved and looked after their children the smarter and stronger those children became. They were strange creatures. At certain times some of them, travelling on those cursed empty whales, had attacked the cetaceans with intent to kill. It was sheer madness, like the males killing the little ones if the females do not defend them.

A female of the land was now swimming close to her. The whale wanted to communicate and tuned her hearing to that stimulus. It was a slow emission if she was afraid, quicker if she felt the maternal femininity that caused an anxious intoxication. A duel of emotions was being built up. The female sea-horse with the forked tail was moving through the water, drawing away from the empty whale which carried her companions. Other cetaceans were swimming in the area but she did not appear frightened. The mother approached softly. Sometimes the sea-horses of the land had accepted help from whales and dolphins.

A memory in her brain was tied to the sea-horses of the land. One of them had approached her: both in the sea, both females. For an instant they were on the same wavelength. The sea-horse had appeared several times, always near one of those empty whales on which it sought refuge. Every so often it transmitted a low whistle, on the frequency that it knew; a confused signal, but a seductive one. The mother felt attracted by that signal and now here it was again.

The female had now drawn very close and the mother left her companions who were some little distance away in order to obtain a clearer reception of the signal which the creature kept transmitting. She had approached her very carefully, moving in the blue water so as to merge with it, trying to behave like one of those empty whales which made the female feel so secure. She had touched her ever so gently, helping her to slither onto her head. The female had let her have her way, readily giving in. The whale, used to communicating over great distances, very clearly heard the transmissions of the female's brain which was so near. She attempted an exchange of energy, as she was in the habit of doing in the depth with other whales, when feminine instinct opened up ever so silently. Before her, another whisper attempted the same exchange. In the blue-coloured thickness other languages hummed, small stimuli, different wave-lengths.

The huge female eased her rhythm so as not to tire the other who was lying on top of her in a state of deep relaxation. Their stories had crossed for an instant, pouring out mysterious memories.

Then time marched on in different ways: for the female sea-horse of the land it ran forward in a linear fashion; for the blue whale it assumed a circular motion.

The whale surfaced in the blinding sun and opened her lungs, sending up a column of spray. In the same instant the female sea-horse of the land slipped away. She was in trouble, like a new-born whale that had just begun to float on the water.

The mother carefully went under again and, sliding under her with utmost delicacy, provided the solid support she was used to on land.

The female rolled into the cavity on the enormous head but was unable to get up. The rocky parasites grappled there gave her something to grip and she hung on as best she could.

She tried to get up again, but was not able. The whale felt herself slipping into drowsiness and once again called out to the female with the same delicacy when, as a mother, she suckled her child.

14

"It's a fantasy, Miriam, a dream."

"No, it's not. I remember it well."

"When you've been through an experience like yours, you do get a bit mixed up."

"But that's how it went."

"So, sometimes, the choice depends on the time and place, not us."

"I can see why you're surprised, Sakty, but listen to my story."

"I'm listening, I'm listening. Still, you've just come out of the coma. You got out of hospital three days ago and you've got to rest. We want you to come back to work as quickly as possible."

"No one's ever talked to a whale before. I've got to try and reconstruct what happened to me."

"You could look at it as a possible interaction between different nervous systems. Here at Trinco we analyse statistical data, photographs; we record sounds, songs – call them what you like. But anything else takes us into the realm of fantasy. A whale that tells the story of her life frankly puzzles me."

"I just want to get to the bottom of all this, that's all. I would like to know if the mother is still around. If so we can try to approach her. All I'm asking you to do is to give me a hand."

"I've got a suggestion, Miriam."

"Let's hear it."

"I'll record the transmission of a blue whale in the bay from the cutter for the time necessary to get a complete set of signals. Then we'll do whatever you like with the data. We'll record over a range of 50/250 Khz. That way you can try out your method."

"Thanks."

"I'll be right in there with you."

"You don't want me to go on my own?"

"Our project has been going for three years. The Marine Council has renewed our permit every year because we have exercised the utmost care and attention. Seeing what's happened to you, we can't send you out to sea on your own for a whole week. It's too dangerous. I'm sorry but I don't intend to let you take the boat out on your own."

"You're not sorry and it's not true you can't let me go on my own. When the statistical project on the whales is completed, there's nothing in my contract that says I can't take other types of observations. I've come here for that too."

Silence reigned on the verandah. It was a morning in May and towards the far end of the bay the sea was marked by a current of violet arabesques. Miriam pursed her lips and looked at the Sinhalese with wavey hair who had helped and directed her during these last months at sea. He reminded her of Felipe, younger, more handsome, but less overbearing. She got up from the chair under the office fan. Outside you could see the seventeenth-century frame of Fort Frederick. In the background a cliff plunged into the sea amidst colours of steel.

Miriam looked at Sakty. They had been working together for a long time and he smiled at her, softening the last words he had said to her. For an instant Miriam felt affection towards him.

"You'll be proud of me."

"With that character of yours? First you throw yourself into the sea against our advice and you very nearly die there. Then all this story. And now your crazy schemes again. How can you work in a team?"

"That's why I'm asking you to let me work on my own. But if it's really necessary you or Anthony can work the boat."

The other assented, uncertain.

"You won't regret it, you'll see."

Sakty went on nodding.

"I understand. It's something which is of more interest to a woman. The search for a lost feeling, social love in the sea."

Sakty began to move his head up and down. It looked like he was saying yes. But he was an Indian and his gesture meant quite the opposite.

15

In the light of the rising sun the dinghy looked like a leaf floating on oil. The hydrophones were in the water. Alex, who had a thorough knowledge of all types of boats and sea beds, was steering with indirect, precise movements. Miriam was in the bow looking through the binoculars. They had come across a school of sperm-whales, males and females, spread over a few miles of sea. The whales beat the water hard and surfaced, twisting their bodies awkwardly, more like islands than animals. They seemed to be resting in preparation for a strenuous communal task.

"They're packing their bags," said Alex.

Miriam tuned the instruments to various frequencies but it wasn't much use; she was looking for her whale through the sudden-changing channels.

"It's going down; let's move on," said Alex.

The tide was going out. They pulled the hydrophones on board and began moving. A thick flight of seagulls was flying in front of the dinghy heading for the place where Miriam's encounter with the mother had occurred. Tension increased as the boat approached the spot. They were drifting in a current that had unexpectedly arisen and was dragging along plankton and slow-swimming fish, followed by others that moved more swiftly. Very clear pools alternated with brush-strokes laden with life like the colours on a palette. Miriam heard the whistling sound in her ear; she took the tiller and headed for an area discoloured in depth.

"The cross-roads," muttered Alex.

It was an area where two currents clashed amidst whirlpools and undercurrents, creating a muddle of bubbles that rose dragging up seaweed and micro-organisms in a saline soup.

Miriam experienced an odd sort of nostalgia on passing over the area and allowed herself to be rocked by the gentle motion. She looked at the sea and felt it was a liquid mother from which she had just come and to which she was ready to return. A ray leapt out of the water, falling back down with a crash. Thousands of rays were rushing in the same direction, together with millions of other transparent, pulsating organisms, both hard and soft. Miriam remembered these vibrations after the encounter with the whale – a lullaby that had bewitched her.

They travelled on for an hour while the shore unfolded like half-closed lips. Four dolphins leapt out of the water, a turtle surfaced to breathe; the fins of two grey nurses marked where the sharks were resting. The sea was a vast bed for every type of wild creature; motionless, it awaited the monsoon of golden sleepiness. Clouds of birds flew above it, up and down without touching the reflecting water. Just under the surface shoals of fish of many colours came within a hair's breath of the airborne life forms. All creatures ready to attack or to flee. In the midst of it all Miriam was travelling on the tacking dinghy, her hair wet with the sea spray.

The boat increased its speed as the hydrophones, below the water line, went on listening.

A reply came: the call of a cetacean. The boat turned, picked up the direction, headed towards it. The sound was following a twisting path because of the currents and the boat traced it. A huge bubble came up from the bottom of the sea.

"This is it," said Alex.

The hydrophones stopped, the motor was turned off and silence reigned. Miriam and Alex leant over the side.

Another bubble came up followed by a low humming, then silence.

The dinghy moved across the water which had just begun to ripple. The land had turned into a yellow-green line that reflected the sunlight. The hydrophones, four metres below the surface, picked up three distant echoes and the boat stopped again. They waited an hour but there was nothing else.

"Let's head back towards land where she appeared and examine the area there," said Miriam.

The boat resumed its journey and whenever an indistinct signal was picked up, Alex stopped the motor to obtain better reception. Nothing. Then a new beating sound was clearly heard. A sperm-whale. A series of warbles made the needles jump as the sun bounced over the horizon and the curtain of night dropped bringing with it sounds, dreams and the pitching of the boat.

The smell of coffee on board heralded the dawn. Alex checked the recordings made during the night but none of the sounds were the ones they were seeking. Frayed clouds announced impending wind. Fine weather for whales, said Alex. The heat of the day brought a stifling calm. The listening devices picked up the passage of tuna and killer whales, everything else was lost in the blue expanse of water. They kept looking through the viewers for hours on end, Miriam stubbornly sustaining that something would appear. The sun ate up the hours.

On the morning of the third day Miriam and Alex were shaken by an enormous huff. They jumped up. A huge sperm-whale broke surface like a square rock. It had a crooked head and huge cross-shaped scars. Its small eyes were fluttering. Miriam was disappointed; so was Alex.

"We're spoilt," he said in a low voice. "We only want your whale."

The dinghy sailed along the right flank of the great beast which was moving its clenched jaw, creating a slight swell. It was a male, unknown to the Trincomalee researchers and had thus never been photographed. It lifted its head, pointing straight towards the sky. Its left eye, rolling among the folds of hard grey skin pitted with parasites and white scars, was black, and had a rigid, indefinably ironic, look about it. The whale remained upright, half out of the water, nosing inquisitively around the dinghy showing no fear. It was thin, its dorsal pads showing, because it was the end of the fasting season. Its back extended beyond the upper fin and a gnash could be seen at the base of the tail which made it seem contorted. It rose up, beating the air, and went under with a splash that rocked the dinghy. Only then did the two researchers feel the blood pulsing in their veins while Miriam's face and arms, burnt by the sun, seemed to have lost their vitality.

Alex looked at her. He shared her adventures and thought that she was favoured by fate although somewhat emotional. He got to work, emptying the dinghy of the water it had taken on board.

"The tape recorders need recharging. We'd best get back to land," said Alex.

"Yes, we'd better get back," echoed Miriam.

Their conversations were quite brief since Alex did not speak much English and she only a little Singhalese.

Miriam pulled up the hydrophones while Alex checked the motor's pump. Silence and emptiness were all around. After a few minutes the motor started up and they headed towards the land.

The next morning they were again at sea and the day after that as well. The sea was absolutely calm and empty; in the haze, flying points of flamingo and shearwater could be made out while the odd dolphin or flying-fish emerged from the water at rare intervals. Miriam waited, face parched by the sun. If she shut her eyes she could see her whale rising from the sea but when she opened them she saw only a few lumps of seaweed floating on the water. She searched for other signs and would have been glad even for the slightest sound, or even at the return of the sperm-whale. Her optimism wavered and she turned to Alex for support. In the clear sky the sun shone murkily; the monsoon was on its way. They continued their search, patiently, night and day. Miriam was absolutely certain that the mother was near. The encounter had changed her, a mysterious exchange had occurred: she felt the gentleness of the enormous animal, and recalled the sense of security experienced on that warm raft. Or had she been mistaken? Had the shock unchained torrents of feeling already present in her brain, non-existent on the outside? She kept feeling the song of the mother, a call that had been grafted in her ear, sweetly, between pauses and pulses.

She waited. At night her sleep was troubled. Nothing happened.

On the evening of the 30th they went back to land.

They tied up at the jetty; their legs folded in a knee-jerk reaction when they jumped to land. The tension had been considerable.

They walked to the office. No one was there; it was the end of the season. They joined their colleagues at the house. The next day the marine observation station closed after a meeting of the staff and a toast – a strange toast since many were missing. It went with the job: moments shared together after long treks in the sea and along the coast in the wake of the whales with the sun beating down. Now they were migrating, but they would return.

They were at the lighthouse and the new custodian,

an agile, excitable Singhalese, did the honours. Felipe had gone away. The new custodian said that a new period of observations began with him. No one quite understood what he meant, but they did not worry too much about it. Miriam, however, felt instinctively that those words meant her relationship with Felipe remained unresolved.

The next day they left for Colombo. After travelling for many hours there was a delay at the Kumbukkanoia River where the bridge was down. They had to take a boat to reach the coast in order to continue beyond Varaz where another river had overflowed its banks and cut the railway line at that point too. The monsoon approaching from the north was making itself felt. The overloaded boat sailed over the troubled sea; the waves made it roll considerably, upsetting the passengers. The group of scientists looked out over the sea: they had spent three months on that stretch of ocean.

Each of them was instinctively looking for something. Miriam's eyes were locked onto a point on the horizon. The others were more relaxed, except for Alex who closely followed Miriam's gaze. Dozens and dozens of passengers were crowded under the awnings which covered the boat's upper deck. Not all were able to stand the crossing; the smell of spices mingled with other, less attractive, smells. A man with lively eyes, unkempt beard, dressed in white pyjamas, was staring at a moving tangle of seaweed where a shoal of fish was feeding. The fish rushed to the boat's wake, agitating the water, when a bucketfull of kitchen waste was thrown overboard and the seaweed was left floating behind, weaving a pattern that stretched in a wake parallel to that of the boat. The Singhalese with the unkempt beard stared at a spot, a metre away, where the water had become quite agitated and saw a sperm-whale break surface and blow. All the other passengers were looking over the other side where the fall of a keg had produced a sudden bang but the man, who was deaf and dumb, had not turned round. So he saw the cetacean and stood still, taking everything in with his eyes. The animal disappeared suddenly, and in its place appeared another, different, cetacean on which a round scar could just be made out. Then it too disappeared and only the seaweed remained, swirling in the whale's wake.

The man had not missed a single detail and opened his mouth to attract the attention of the other passengers but stopped abruptly as he felt that somehow the whale was looking for someone. He smiled, knowing that only very few people understood that language. The other passengers had not seen anything; one of them turned towards the railing, but did not see what had happened. The man tried, through the use of gestures, to tell his travelling companion who simply shrugged, used as he was to the man's eccentric behaviour. He then approached the group of scientists and attempted to pass on the message received, but was rewarded with their condescending smiles, including Miriam's, although she had heard something, a whistling sound. She did not pay much attention, following the gestures of the man who was pointing at the sea, miming a fish surfacing then diving, followed by another huge animal. She thought she understood and attempted to tell him, imitating his gestures, and he repeated the mime. They stood there, staring at each other, lost in thought, then Alex came up and said the man was from Batticaloa, had been in the hospital at the same time she was there, had seen her and knew her story. The man, encouraged, again mimed the whale launching its message, but now Miriam had adopted a condescending attitude as she thought he was referring to the story of her encounter in the sea. Assuming she had understood, he dragged the woman to the railing, indicating the point where the whale had made her appearance. Miriam smiled at him; the man resembled Felipe. He tried to tell her that her whale had come to the boat, to look for her but neither Miriam nor the others understood.

16

"It was total darkness for him."

"It's always dark inside the belly."

"Jonah was a prophet, he must have seen something."

"He saw through time, like all the prophets."

"Well, the haruspex looked in the stomachs of the animals to predict the future, Felipe."

"And you, a missionary priest, go round telling these stories!"

"What do you know about how Jonah saw?"

"I don't know anything. But I've come here especially to ask you something, since you study all types of prophets, great and not so great."

"Jonah must have picked up something. He was in the belly for three days."

"In the mouth."

"Well, inside, anyway."

"The same thing happened to a sailor, fifty years ago in the Atlantic. He ended up in a whale's mouth, then was spat out, reduced to an imbecile."

"I've read it in the Nantucket chronicles."

"Was Jonah reduced to idiocy too?"

"That I haven't read. He continued his work, but became quite short-tempered. Like you are sometimes, Felipe."

"Biblical history is keeping something from us."

"Biblical history is where we all come from. It's the popularization of the first words: *Word, Chaos, Abraham, Leviathan*. That's how we started to think. But you want to know if a whale can carry a man? Yes, if he's a bit crazy. Otherwise it can't."

"As far as I'm concerned there's a woman involved."

"Then it's different."

The priest looked out from the verandah over the port of Galle, in the south of Sri Lanka. Felipe was searching for Miriam; he wanted her again. But the whale, the mother, had come between them. So Felipe had gone away and after wandering about he had come to Galle to see his friend Jan, a missionary.

"The relationship between woman and nature is one big muddle," said Jan.

"What's it to do with Jonah?"

"Jonah is the man who loses himself in woman, in nature. If he manages to come out of it well, a new man is born. It's different for a woman; it's a return to a dimension, to a language of the beginning."

Jan was panting. He was fat with a pinkish face and eyes like those of a ferret. He worked with a Dutch evangelical mission. "The whale is the primeval mother, warm, but without words. We've got to search for her, to communicate with her in order to discover a sense of belonging, to find out where we come from. Perhaps it's easier for a woman."

"So a woman is more likely to make some sense out of all this mess than a man?"

"The truth of the matter is that you want the woman and all she can think of is the whale."

"So?"

"So you haven't come to ask me to play the part of the pimp, have you?"

They laughed.

"Didn't we use to go after women together once?" said Felipe.

"That was a long time ago. Now you go on your own. But all this woman wants is to search for love."

"A woman is always looking for love, whether it's sons or lovers," said Felipe. "But I'm after trying to understand women and whales."

"In Hawaii a linguist has constructed two like languages to communicate with two female dolphins. One is made up of gestures which the dolphin follows from the water and to which she replies. The other consists of a series of whistles and whimpers that become words. They've built up a vocabulary of fifty words with which it's possible to compose hundreds of utterances."

"I know that," Felipe cut in.

"Yes, you know everything about dolphins. Try and find out from your friend if it's the same with the whales. Speak to her."

"She won't tell me anything. I've tried, but it's useless."

"So suprise her. Organize a trip to follow the migrations of the whales, for example. It's quite feasible in this day and age with those electronic tracking gadgets."

"And this would be serendipity?"

"I don't know. The Book of Jonah ends like this: 'Should I not be moved by a city where there are thousand of innocent animals?' The Lord had a deep emotional attachment to animals. Maybe it's the same for your friend. Women have a natural gift for this sort of language."

"I'm interested in the relationship between the whale and humankind, in what they can say to each other. I remember it was great with the dolphins, but I understand less about whales. And I understand people who do research on whales even less. I've lived with them at the lighthouse for a month or so. They seem to be exploring a world of their own."

"Why?"

"They come and go like the whales. At the end of the season they go back home, to Europe or America. Or they follow the whales to the Poles. Some go to Argentina, Australia or California. There's about a hundred groups like this. Wanderers; here one year, on the other side of the world the next. Usually they go after the same whales they know personally, almost as if they were their oceanic double. Strange types – you meet up with them unexpectedly in another ocean. They get involved with you for a week, a month, then disappear for years, or for ever. A strange kind of breed who wants to talk to the whales."

"The whale was once seen as representing chaos, as a monster. Now that it tries to communicate with man, it's no longer so. Chaos means not to communicate, not to talk. Evil, the monster, has gone over to the other side, to a man who does not try to talk, to understand. You've got to try, though. Your woman's trying."

"What do I have to do?"

"Search in the heart of the whale and in that of the woman."

17

One of the legends of Sakaman Lagoon tells the story of a whale that comes to pray on the beach because she wants to become a woman and a mother again, as she was in the long distant past. But the men she speaks to will not allow it. Only the women of the place can intercede since they know a very ancient language, a language spoken only by women and whales, or at least by those who have shared the experience of bringing up a little one. The women learnt it by going down to the beach where every so often a cetacean runs aground and they try to help it return to the sea or to die.

There is a ceremony where the women urge the men to grant the whale's prayer. Dressed in sarongs striped like a whale's stomach, the women on the beach mime the dance performed by the huge animals as they approach the shore. Two bamboo boats with palm leaf frames are pushed into the sea to represent the whale. On the last waves of the tide, beyond the coral barrier where the calm water reflects the light of the coconut oil lamps, the animal brings peace and love. The men watch, suspicious and uncertain, from the shore.

The passage of a whale during the festival is considered a sign of good luck and of the sea's pleasure. The women go into the water and offer the great sea mother little boats made of coconut shells filled with food and flowers. The false whale built for the festival is pushed ashore and destroyed. Women come out of its huge belly symbolising the return to human form according to the legend.

Miriam watched the ceremony from the shore. She had asked if she could take part and they had told her to wait at the edge of the beach and to come forward when the women came out of the sea. The first woman that from the shore heads towards the hills becomes queen of the festival. Thus Miriam was made queen for that year.

Miriam had gone home, to Australia, during the monsoon season and after had returned to Sri Lanka to carry on with her research. She still wanted to find the mother who had been sighted a number of times in the vicinity.

The mother was recognisable by the way the eyes were set at the sides of her head and by the scars on the dorsal fin where she had been bitten by the killer whales. She had joined a group of blue whales made up of young and very young females that was cruising up and down the coast. When the time came they would be heading for the open sea in search of the marine channel where the currents marked the way to the south pole. There are certain hidden waterways used by the whales which pass close to few islands and cover vast expanses of open sea and they head for the icy pastures of the south only when they have found their mysterious channel, often seeking it for a long time.

The mother appeared to a Sakaman woman the day after the festival of the sea. She surfaced, her snout lengthened, not far from a fishing boat. The woman noticed that there were other females with a herd of little ones and a few young males not far from land. They were splashing about, playing, diving, throwing up columns of vapour, looking just like a fleet of steamships about to cast anchor. The mother approached the shore, the water pouring from her sides, through the crustaceans stuck on her head. Her spoon-shaped mouth opened with a sucking gesture, the upper lip vibrating almost as though she were calling out for attention. Most of her body was under water. As she turned over on her side the outline of the eye behind the jaw became visible and thus she was recognised.

The closeness of the whale caused a stir of excitement among a group of women washing mats in the sea. They knew Miriam's story so they sent for her but, when she came a couple of hours later, the mother had already gone to join her companions in an area where the sea bed was rich with plankton and crustaceans, and seaweed formed speckled patterns. The whales' backs shone in the sunlight like smooth rocks.

Miriam got into the blue rowing boat and headed for the group of cetaceans that came up and went under like the pistons of an underwater machine. The woman approached the snouts which just broke the surface of the water but was not able to make out the mother. The animals were still, silent. A little one came near, while two adults placed themselves on either side of the boat. Miriam felt as though she were being scrutinised by the eyes of ancestors come out of a long sleep. The shore in the background underwent a transformation: the forests became taller; the women washing the mats changed into striped otters tearing just-captured fish. Miriam pulled hard on the oars and the scene returned to normal. She headed for the open sea, searching for her whale, her arms taut with the effort of rowing. All around everything was coloured in a shade of deep blue, from her dress to the backs of the whales under the sparkling sky. Miriam felt the whistling sound in her ear and bent down to prepare the hydrophones for immersion. When she lifted her head to lower them into the water, the mother was in front of her, transfixed in the glaring light of the sun.

Miriam's gaze wandered over the enormous, semi-submerged head where a faintly impudent smile mocked the slightness of her frame. It was the look of an inaccessible world, that of a huge sea goddess who had appeared from the depths. The oars were stuck to Miriam's hands. She felt like a butterfly fallen into the sea, her wings stiffened, while the giant observed her among the fresh pungent smell of fish. A baby whale surfaced nearby, squealing. The boat slowly approached the trembling mouth. The head seemed to have been hurt in forcing open a mysterious gate. The mother came from the deep valleys of the planet and gave out a smell of sulphur and lemons. Her motionless eye rolled geometrically in the silence interrupted by the barely audible lapping of the fins.

The whale's body trembled ever so slightly as Miriam

placed her hand on her head. A momentary shiver ran down her spine and she felt that time stood still. An indefinable feeling took hold of her as she began to speak in a whisper.

"I've been looking for you," she murmured.

The whale gave no sign; only her eye kept rolling.

The woman repeated the sounds she had recorded, a series of rhythmic puffs which she realized were incongruous. She felt a sudden laugh rising and attempted to stifle it. A sigh tightened the pit of her stomach. The mother did not move. Miriam withdrew her hand and rowed to the mouth. In the grip of a strange frenzy she began to hit out at the parasitic crustaceans stuck to the lips; the mother observed without reacting as her hands were being scratched in the attempt. Then she looked up and saw the rock-like parasites in the hollow of the head, in front of the blowholes where she had clung that day in the sea off Trincomalee. The parasitic crustaceans had helped her and they were much too small to bother an animal like the whale. She placed her hands on the cetacean's skin, next to the eye. A shiver went through her as though in reply.

Miriam spoke softly. It was an outburst, a monologue that had undertones of irony and of prayer, pouring desires and disappointments over the head of the animal. She created words similar to the sounds uttered by the whales, mixing them with words of her own, forming unexpected rhymes. The vibrations in the mother's skin increased whenever Miriam stopped talking. The cetacean was intensely blue and that gave her strength. She moved gradually around the head. All fear had gone; her only concern was that the mother might go under thus putting an end to the encounter. Her arms stretched out in an incongruous attempt to embrace the whale as she pronounced a name, a sound, mzir, mzir that she had heard the mother utter repeatedly. She would have given anything to obtain a reply, even the strangest one. The monologue continued, fragmented by calls and bizarre gestures. The eye of the mother moved towards Miriam who became aware of the movement and stepped back to enter the animal's field of vision. The eye seemed to notice it but there was no other reply. The woman moved closer and began to rub the whale's skin, receiving vibrations in return. She continued rubbing for a minute or so, but time had lost all meaning. The other whales were far away. So were the people on the beach. Suddenly Miriam noticed that they had begun rotating, one in front of the other.

They were forming a two-petal daisy pattern.

18

The boat and the mother circled in a slow whirlpool. With its oars up the little boat looked like a butterfly. The huge mouth vibrated ever so slightly with a jerking kind of motion, the eyes set at the back like two watch-towers. Miriam was talking as though she were addressing a child or an elderly person, concentrating on the tone of voice more than the words and reproducing the sounds recorded through the hydrophones. It was she who was the mother now communicating with an unknown creature that had come from an unreal dimension.

The whale was motionless, its lip touching the boat, softly, sweetly.

The two floated in the ocean a few hundred metres from shore like an asymmetric corolla that had fallen in the water. A sudden shower covered the boat; Miriam was startled, fear returned and disappeared in words indistinctly murmured. Silence reigned once more.

Now the whale had become a slow-moving submarine looking through its periscopes. Miriam was stunned by strange mental associations: she was on the petal of an impossible flower in a unexplored meadow. The woman dipped the oars in the water and moved along the whale's flank. She found a song of blue whales on the tape and played it to the giant in front of her. The mother's skin trembled; Miriam was trembling too. She went up to the eye and tried to send signals made up of light and shadow, striking it with the hand. The pupil reacted with a gluey pulsation and the woman kept her hand firmly on the socket. The mother did not move and Miriam resumed her whispered monologue, knowing there would not be another chance. The dance continued like that of a bee around a flower unwilling to give up its pollen. The two females were slowly drifting towards the open sea. They were too near to each other, too dazed, too silent. The mother's head slowly sank and she disappeared without causing a ripple. Miriam was alone; the ocean was completely empty as far as the eye could see. She collapsed in the bottom of the slowly-rotating boat and began to cry.

When Miriam got up, sharp-winged birds were flying in the sky above. She began to row towards the shore.

She pulled the boat onto the empty beach, tying it to a pole stuck in the dry sand, took the tape recorder and headed up the path towards Marion's bungalow, the Singhalese teacher with whom she was staying. In front of the house was the half-destroyed paper whale, used for the festival. Miriam went up to it and touched the carcass; the wind was making it vibrate, like the skin of the mother in the sea. "I'm drunk," she muttered; she felt hot all over, an increasing malaise. As soon as she went in, Marion helped her to bed without saying a word. It had been a strange day.

"I saw you coming from the beach."

"I'm thirsty."

"I'll make some tea."

Marion had a round child-like face. She served tea and some food on a mat depicting mythological scenes. They ate, recalling the experience Marion had gone through – her friend had been watching from the shore. Marion told her something about the arrival of the whales.

"When they get here they are silent," she said. "It's the fasting season. They don't eat and communicate little."

"Perhaps they don't want to," said Miriam sadly.

"They're curious about the land and need silence. The women know."

"What do the men say?"

"They laugh. They like the ceremony, the one with the queen. But that's about as far as it goes. They don't care."

"What do you think?"

"Same as you."

"I'm scared again now. I don't know why."

"Something similar happened years ago to the queen of the festival."

"Tell me."

"I don't know if it was the same whale. Must have been ten years ago, in October, just like now."

"With a whale that left the herd?"

"A female, smaller than this one."

"Did the queen go out to meet her?"

"In an outrigger. Alone, like you did."

"What happened?"

"She went out in the cove west of the one you took. We watched from the beach. The whale just quitely swam round the boat and the girl touched it."

"Then what?"

"She told us that they faced each other in silence just like you. At first the girl couldn't utter a sound, then she started to sing and the whale swam round in circles. A merry-go-round. It was a curious animal; it dived and surfaced many times. Then the girl went away, frightened; the whale floated on the surface for a bit, then dived and went away."

"Where's the girl now?"

"She left. I don't know where she went."

"Does anybody know?"

"I don't know."

"But what do they say about these things here?"

"I told you. The men laugh and the women don't say anything. It's a weird story. We think it's an exchange, a sort of return to the beginning of time. Now I remember. That woman said that the mothers try to communicate something long since lost."

"Who to?"

"Other mothers."

"But I'm not a mother."

"Maybe that's why the whale didn't talk to you."

"Did this happen to the other queen too?"

"She wasn't a mother either. Maybe these are just old wives' tales."

"Doesn't a woman who is also a mother ever go to sea?"

"No. They're afraid."

"Well, what can we do then?"

The Singhalese woman shrugged, tilting her head slightly to say that it was a mysterious world. Better not talk too much about it.

"Maybe a mother would understand?" asked Miriam.

They both smiled. It was a crazy sort of conversation,

but Miriam felt better. She went out, saying she needed some air, now that night was falling. Outside the paper whale was still flapping in the breeze and Miriam sat down next to it. Two women joined her. They sat in silence, casting furtive glances around.

Further away a woman was nursing a child in the doorway of a hut. Miriam went down to the beach, to the boat, but did not launch it since it was late. She sat, contemplating the view. In the distance the sound of waves breaking over the coral reef could be heard. She had to decide whether to go back to work on the project or follow her own lead right to the end. They would say she was mad but there was no other choice: carry on or forget it. Someone was trying it in Hawaii and was being mocked by most people.

Marion, the Singhalese woman, came up to her and spoke for a bit about other things. A flock of birds fluttered overhead.

"When a huge warm-blooded animal leaves the equator and travels towards the pole, it somehow restricts its world in order to survive and evolve. The island women who go inside the paper whale sing this story and become part of it."

Miriam found Marion's tale enchanting. She looked at her friend who had made-up eyes, a puffy face and a mouth like that of a duck. Marion retold the legend of the cetacean that wanted to become human and return to the land, adding that the whales speak only where they feel the bitter cold.

Then she fell silent. Evening had turned into night.

"In the seas of ice," Marion said after a while, "there are rivers of animals that spell life for the whales. Rivers, lakes, seas of minute crustaceans for kilometres and kilometres on end."

She turned to her motionless companion.

"Perhaps there you can talk to the whales. That's where there's a little crustacean they eat. Krill, it's called."

19

"Krill. krill. krill."

The shout echoed everywhere. A cover of feathers was spreading over the sea as flights of birds dived into the water after food. Penguins were leaping about in the sea like dolphins. The bay was dotted with little icebergs and swept by the waves which crashed against the tall ice cliffs of the shore. A pearly mist hung over the white-rimmed black cauldron seething with krill, billions of minute crustaceans of ever-changing colours. The animals were gathered for an oceanic Bacchanal, each one devouring the other, right down to the krill who fed on the diatom in the plankton. The young krill floated on the surface, the adults stayed under water and in the middle swam the open-mouthed whales.

Two slim ships on the horizon completed the picture. Two large lifeboats had been launched and were advancing amid the splashing water. Rose-coloured waves rose in every direction.

"Krill, krill," the shout echoed among yells and screeches. Albatross, skua and stormy petrels were swept about by the gusts of wind; seals and whales leapt in the water. All sorts of animals appeared in and over the sea; they had converged here from all directions and were rushing about, jaws wide open. All forms of life were engaged in an intense paroxysm, except for the fish, which were almost an absent quality. There were only a few cod, whose blood did not freeze since it could withstand the cold.

"Krill, krill," the shout was lost behind a boat on the

crest of a wave which went down into the trough, coming up again immediately. Its hooded crew lowered instruments and harpoons in the water, pulling them up in haste. There were about ten boats, some long with rigging like steel spider's webs, others squat and made of rubber. The former fished, the latter belonged to a conservationist organization that was keeping an eye on the fishermen to prevent excessive catches and subsequent depletion. The two groups had met up a few days ago and the former had tried to get away from the latter. Now the confrontation continued on the boats.

"Krill, krill." The shout drew men and animals together, blending with the roar of the engines. In the troubled water, light and shadow cut across countless wakes.

The animals moved about in ever-increasing frenzy. The boats tried to spread out as the rubber dinghies darted among them like maddened bees. The largest of the ships, a red one, headed for the middle of the corrida. The krill, divided in red-coloured rivers, headed towards the steep cliffs. Black dominated the lower parts, blue the upper ones, in the middle lay the strip of glaciers. The whales devoured everything in their path, spurting fountains of water in return, between swings of tails and sudden dives; tons of krill ended up in the whales' mouths as they were still eating the last of the diatom and the odd penguin also met its end in the jaws of the cetaceans. A grey whale headed for the approaching ship and two boats veered to avoid colliding with it as it dived, reappearing in the wake of the ship amidst the teeming krill. A pipe lowered from the ship was sucking up the food supply and the whale hit at it, sending small crustaceans flying in all directions to the applause of the conservationists in the rubber boats. Wind and wave created confusion everywhere as life bounced from stomach to stomach becoming lumps of food. The skeleton of a penguin floated nearby, a few feathers still stuck to it and minute crustaceans hiding under the bones picked clean by a seal. This feast recurred every spring, consummated in the bodies seeking energy in the icy cold, while the whales ploughed through the krill in all directions as the polar banquet went on.

In the crystal clear air Miriam pulled two probes out of the water and handed Felipe a harpoon. They were together again, working with a group of researchers from Australia on board the red ship. They had different tasks: Felipe analysed the krill eaten by the animals he captured; Miriam studied the concentration of the krill banks at different depths.

"This is a woman's harpoon!" exclaimed Felipe as he threw it away.

"Are you saying that because you didn't manage to spear the cod?" Miriam asked ironically.

"Hand me the other one, it's better."

"But will you manage?"

The two had resumed their relationship, angrily, arguing continuously. During the day they were always in the boat with their instruments; at night the cold kept them close together. Now, in the water teeming with life, they observed a boat approaching. It belonged to another ship.

"The Greenpeace crowd is on to us. They don't trust us," said the skipper, a black-bearded Argentine.

"But we're all here to save the whales," objected Felipe. "We're riding herd on them, together in a common cause. What are they scared of?"

A puff of wind threw krill in their faces. Miriam wiped her glasses and looked up; there was krill everywhere. On her glove a little prawn curled up and slipped away; the eyes were the only black spots on the minute rose-coloured animal. All around there were other minute eyes. Between sun and ice the world was the colour of blood. One ship was lowering tubes to suck up the reddish vortex, the other ordered its boats to interfere with the operation. Two whales surfaced between the ships, blowing.

It was the last day of harvest at Weddell and tension was at its peak. They all noticed it: the animals swam, disappearing into the teeming krill; the men moved frenziedly. In the middle of it all Miriam measured the concentrations, lowering grading bags into the sea. Beside her, Felipe was catching a sort of bony ice fish, the only variety of fish native to the place. His beard stuck out of a blue bonnet spotted with red.

Miriam was weighing a lump of krill when she suddenly stopped short. A whale had surfaced in front of the boat, bending its back in a flurry of foam and churning krill with its tail. Behind it another one was doing the same thing. Neither of the two was the mother Miriam had met in the warm seas, and she swore. Felipe turned to look at her for an instant, with an ironic grimace, then went back to his fishing.

Ice and icebergs were lit up by a beam of sunlight on the horizon, and the sky shone yellow and red over the boats spread out like a fan in the dark sea. All around them, with matching frenzy, the animals carried on with the hunt.

The skua glided down on the sea or on the boats, their beaks dripping red, and were driven away by the men. Petrels and albatross cruised above suddenly diving into the water around the boats which moved in an increasingly irregular manner becoming dirtier by the minute. The krill that was devoured invaded and swallowed up its predators, transforming the scene enclosed by the milky spires of the glaciers rising from the sea.

Miriam rubbed her ears, hearing the whistling sound return, and looked for the mother. She thought she saw her several times among the whales that could just be made out next to the glaciers – the same scars, the same painted eyes. But she wasn't certain and the hours fled with the sun.

At sunset group of whales surfaced all together, blowing, heading for the mouth of the bay.

"They're off to Esperance, the blue whales' favourite strait," said Felipe. That's where we'll find them."

Night came down on the boats as they returned to the ship; krill mush went on flowing in the water, among increasingly invisible seals and penguins. Miriam put away the scales and went to join her companions, who were warming themselves and drinking coffee from a thermos. The mother had not appeared; she was hiding under the river of crustaceans, perhaps some distance away, beyond Weddell Bay, under one of those white-oozing mountains that rose in the west. Two boats that had delayed their return came in. The wind was dying down; shouts and calls had ceased with the setting of the sun. The boat crews spoke of the last group of whales sighted.

"It's the Sri Lanka 'school,' I regognized them. Same scars as last year. They're creatures of habit; they come back to the same pastures."

"And the mother?" asked Miriam.

"The old ones go off first; they prefer the young krill beyond Esperance."

"They gather in Gerlach Canal. They're safe there."

The man who had spoken was a Scot, thick beard, deep-set eyes. He had researched in the area for years.

"How many have you catalogued?" asked Felipe.

"Blues?"

"Yes."

"About thirty. One or two new ones are added every year."

"And the mother?"

"They also call her the whale with the painted eye, because of the round spot on her head. She sends out a considerable quantity of signals to make the others follow her. A real matriarch."

"What do the conservationists say? Have they sighted her?"

"We haven't talked to them much. The mother's even more receptive in the cold water, far as I know."

"Does she show herself much?"

"It's different from the warmth of the tropics."

"I met her in warm water," said Miriam.

"So I've heard."

"They tell me it's easy to sight her."

"We reckon she goes to Gerlach before the others, in the fiord where the Chilean base is."

"She's based around the Cuverville pastures, the island without ice cliffs, more to the south."

"A beautiful place. We'll go there in a few days."

20

Two free-floating icebergs almost closed off the entrance to Gerlach Canal like enormous watch dogs. The ice-breaker squeezed in between the two floating masses, and headed towards the arm in the direction of the island of Cuverville. It was the equinox of the southern autumn and in a few days the ice would cut off the Antarctic peninsular where the whales come to search out the last meal of summer.

The icebergs hung a blue canopy over the ocean. A tangle of fog blotted out the landscape, cutting sheer-sided mountains; mountain tops towered above the fog. Penguins scurried over the huge slabs of ice floating on the sea.

The icebreaker picked its way among the perils of the deep, following the line of the sheer-sided mountains, navigation after sunset guided by the light of the moon. The absolute stillness of mountain peaks and water gave a sense of uniqueness to the scene. All life seemed to have vanished. They reached their island destination, Cuverville. The ship cast anchor and a boat was launched with eight people on board. A huge whale had been sighted.

Miriam slid down the left side of the boat and sat down, hanging onto the gunwale. An instant later the boat set out. The bottom of the canal was a light blue colour, the rocky cliffs of Cuverville and Ronge, the island nearby, stood out tall, yellow with ice on the top. The boat was towing two smaller boats. New icebergs appeared, forming a second scene, a sort of cloister inside the amphitheatre of ice, the fiord dissolving in the background. A pack of penguins came out of the water, clambering onto the wind-streaked ice. On every side sheer-sided cliffs made navigation difficult. The huge immaculate forms led to a cave grotto wadded in fog that thinned out at a black peak.

"The mountain is called Royal. The climate changes here," someone in the boat said.

Miriam was experiencing a strange sort of elation, a familiar sound ringing in her ear. A shape came out of the water; hump opened up among a crackling wave; a puff of air dissipated amidst the mountains; an iceberg tipped over. Waves rocked the boat violently and everyone grabbed hold of what they could. Behind the boat an enormous head was surfacing, growing bigger and bigger as it came out of the sea. It opened its mouth on the waterline and Miriam felt her heart beat faster. It was the great whale.

The woman jumped into the little boat tied behind. She set down the tape recorder and grabbed the oars without an instant's hesitation. The lifeboat kept its distance, moving in an arc so as not to interfere with the manoeuvre. The others knew about Miriam's relationship with the cetacean.

The whale disappeared and came up again, sliding on her side so as not to make waves. Then she headed for the ice cliff wall of Mount Royal. In her haste to communicate, Miriam whispered something. The icebergs spaced apart and the islands of Ronge and Cuverville appeared, dotted with birds in flight. The sky was streaked with rose that changed to green. The Antarctic was showing its colours.

Miriam turned as she rowed. The sound in her ear changed in intensity, becoming a syllabic nuance. Her enormous companion was leading her towards the fog-wrapped cliff wall. The woman went on rowing, turning around, as the mother showed her painted eye, brushing past a wall between arches and seracs. Outside the larger boat was following the same route under the ever-changing light of the moon.

Skua were flying about in the sky. Little by little everything fell silent. Miriam stared at the painted eye just above the waterline, then at the real eye set at the corner of the mouth. A voice hit her.

"You've come."

"What?" she exclaimed.

The voice did not speak and the woman looked at the shape floating beside her.

"What's happening?" she whispered.

There was no reply. The sky was clearing.

The mother scraped along the ice wall, heading for a

nearby cave, lit from the inside. She swam into a long tunnel and Miriam followed. The light became bluish and things could not be seen clearly as very small icebergs broke off the walls, floating free. Neither current nor cold came from that place. Miriam let go of the oars and called out in a low voice. The mother was proceeding along the ice tunnel and had taken on a bluish tinge. She banged into a wall which disintegrated and the undertow broke into a sluggish wave that rocked the boat and vanished into silence.

The animal banged into the wall again. Then it began to get bigger, until it filled up the whole cave. The white glare increased while a deep blue reflection flooded the water. The lake pulsated slightly. Something flew overhead, but the reflection ate up the image. The animal went under and Miriam, frightened, turned the boat around to go back, but she could not make out the entrance to the cave, which must have been nearby. The light left everything in suspense, even the body of the whale which began to speak.

"You've come."

Miriam heard the phrase again, or at least she thought she did. She resumed her rowing, looking for the entrance. The voice spoke for the third time. Miriam made sure that the tape recorder was working. Perhaps it was a joke played by her colleagues. But she was uneasy.

"We can talk," it said.

The water had become pale-blue dotted with reddish spots. A small cloud of krill surfaced, crackling lightly. In the ensuing silence Miriam asked instinctively:

"Is this the place where the mothers come? A place of the origins?"

"A place of the origins."

"But where are you? Why don't you show yourself?"

The tape recorder kept whirring; Miriam checked it,

the sound flowed normally, providing a sense of real time. All else was enchantment.

The mother grew bigger and bigger and went round in ever tightening circles. The cave was small and the enormous animal fitted like a glove, her dorsal fin pointing upwards. As she circled, her eyes showed one at a time and Miriam tried to look into them. A light shone out of them. It seemed as though the place was filled with eyes and Miriam was reassured. A host of images rushed out to her from the opaque whiteness. The whale was there. Miriam spoke to reassure herself.

"Do you come here? Do the whales come here, before giving birth?"

There was no reply but she felt herself dissolving, going into the water, swimming towards the huge figure in front of her. Another cloud of krill appeared as the metamorphosis of colours continued. The scene expanded and turned into a painting in ice.

"It's a quiet place," she heard. Or perhaps she said it.

The fin began to circle again like a flag around the little boat in the centre of the ever-tightening cave. The eye of the mother ran on; it was the focal point of a dimension Miriam had just entered. The fog dispersed as the whale vanished. Overhead the sun shone in rose-tinted glare.

The little boat rocked and Miriam held the tape recorder tightly, making sure that it was working. She stopped it, changed the tape, took a deep breath and listened; she heard a gurgling sound. Laughter welled up inside her for the absurd situation she was in. The little lake was trembling. The machine kept recording as the mother swam round in circles, then began speaking again in a barely discernible whisper.

The voice was not produced by the vocal chords. It came from the bottom of the throat where sounds were sights, eyes were smells and the motion of the tail language, as though the senses were fused in a single sensory channel in which living beings lived and laughed. Laughter was seriousness, physical strength love, the dance in the water transmuted into music. Creatures ready to help, loaded with intensity, communicated through their united senses. It was a language that had already been heard, the story Miriam had learned in the equatorial sea, the story of the creature which united past and present. In the sea the whales called to each other very frequently and over great distances, but there was another barrier they still had to overcome: communication with other species. Miriam felt her elation concentrate in a question.

"How can that happen?"

She felt a sense of wonder and placed a hand on her stomach. The noise of the tape recorder made her nervous and she stopped it. The whale became small again, a blue dot in the white hue that invaded the cave; her fin stood still in the water. Miriam turned on the tape recorder again speaking of the haste displayed by humans. This puzzled the whales since they had come to the end of their evolutionary circle and were awaiting the final phase before dissolving in the colour of infinity.

Something twisted inside the tape recorder. It stopped and Miriam worked for a while trying to fix it with her fingers. She wanted to laugh.

"What's the matter with me?" she mumbled. Miriam repeated the words, stammering, asking for help as something penetrated her eye. It was a look that came from the surface of the water, embracing everything, settling on the cliff walls of the lake, on the little boat, on every surface. The whistling sound came back into Miriam's ear, sweetly, like the memory of a forgotten melody. The whale in the water grew larger, eyes rolling, skin suddenly able to hear, as though it had become an organ able to receive and transmit anywhere. The whistling sound mingled, mixed with the noise of the rope beating the water.

"Shak, shar, ashar, astrar."

The cliff walls echoed the sounds, the tape recorder registered them and the blue figure was swallowed up by the light. The sounds became acoustic waves that formed utterances not generated by thought.

Miriam began to row round the whale. On the sea bed a group of penguins swam noiselessly. Each creature was part of a whole; a unique ecosystem pulsated in the ice. Krill, plankton, diatoms, penguins and fish able to lower the freezing point of their blood were all born there. Now the penguins were dancing. Miriam would have liked her colleagues to be present but they were waiting outside the cave, having given up the pursuit. The whales won't talk to us, they said smiling ironically, at most they sing for love, like the birds.

Now the whale seemed small. She opened her mouth and began to grow again as krill and penguins beat on the water. Her mouth became enormous. Fear returned. Miriam decided to row away and turned rapidly towards the exit but the ice blinded all detail; the elements were all mixed up. The mother had again grown to an immense size; she alone moved, slowly, using her tail: gestures for other senses.

She continued to dance on the water, then lost her colour, dived, shrunk to a point.

Miriam was alone. She played back the tape recorder, noticing a warm stream weaving among the succession of short words and sounds. The cetacean surfaced again, opening and shutting her mouth, becoming larger and larger. She went right up to the little boat, then dived.

Surfacing on the other side, she brushed past the boat

without touching it. Miriam did not move. The eye of the whale stared at her as the whale's heart beat heavily under the skin. Something in the water pulsated as one with Miriam, a rhythmic unison between beings who sought to communicate with each other, finding a time in common. The woman felt the rhythm spread throughout her body. She burst into hysterical laughter, became frightened, called out for help. The mother continued diving, soundlessly; only her heartbeat could be heard as her tail spun. It was the dance of the whales for one of their kind in difficulty. Miriam, in the boat, was going round in circles, shouting and flailing about with the oars. A whistling sound was heard similar to the one in her ear, and her heart leapt in her throat. She turned on the tape recorder to record what was happening. The whale's heartbeat now echoed loudly under the roof of ice.

The whale was enormous but at the same time comical. She stopped in front of the little boat, her mouth shut. For an instant Miriam thought she was laughing. She had noticed many times in the pictures of whales a grimace that looked like a stifled laugh. She remembered their first meeting in the tropics, in the lagoon. Her mouth had been shut.

Miriam stretched her hand towards the whale's muzzle, but the cetacean gently went under. The blue fin came up on the other side of the boat, followed by the wash of the tail.

"It's the dance for communicating with a different type of creature, the last farewell of a species at the end of its cycle. The mother belongs to a race about to become extinct. It's like a swan song," said Miriam into the microphone.

She switched off the tape recorder. The whale had gone under without a sound. Further away an ice wall slid into the water and the ripples spread out until they reached the boat, making it rock for a few seconds. The collapse of the wall revealed glass-like rivulets; it looked like the stomach of an unknown creature. Images and shapes etched by the water in the transparent walls took on a life of their own. The whale was in the middle. She represented an ancient story of intense cold and geometry. The eyes of the cetacean, the real ones or the one etched into the skin by past struggles, shone tersely, forming a fantastic, splendid face that dominated all other elements. The cheeks were flooded with slits, twisting in a grimace that looked like an emerging smile. The light on the huge face grew more intense. Below, a little whale bloomed in the lap of the thousand-eyed creature.

It was a phenomenon of these latitudes where the whales came to confirm their pregnancy, in a place where the resistance of a warm-blooded animal was pushed to the limits. Perhaps pregnancy was for an instant interrupted in that mysterious tranquillity where colours and the rhythm of life blended with the colours and rhythms of the sea. Miriam allowed herself to be carried off; the whale was pushing the boat rather than dragging it along in her wake. The flowing waters had caused part of the wall to collapse, revealing an unexpected sight that juxtaposed the most primitive elements of nature with the most evolved. The cold was intense. Miriam resumed recording and called the mother again, pronouncing her name as though it indicated the characteristics of the species rather than that of the creature before her. The freezing cold had etched the scene in the water, where a mother had come to hear the origins of the rhythm that would have brought a new being to life, a being that would be born only if it could survive the dance in the extreme cold.

The hum of the machine blended with the lapping sound made by the mother as she pushed the boat. It was like a game. Miriam had done it once in the pool with dolphins. The same help, the same dancing push. She wanted to hug the whale's muzzle, but it was impossible. She heard the whale sing a whispered song, almost as if she were weeping because unable to express herself. She towered above her, blind, with the quiet strength of someone who can accept anything to allow another smaller creature to live, whether of the same or of a different species, willing to withstand any trial in order to find a common language, even if only made up of vibrations, transformed into a wild dance as they increase.

Miriam's heart jumped in her throat. She felt useless and happy. At that very moment the mother hit the little boat, hurling it in the air.

A swirl of water swept the woman towards the cave entrance as the whale's tail disappeared noisily under water.

Two hands hoisted the dripping girl onto the big boat amid shouts and curt commands. The tape recorder strapped to her chest was intact and dripping. Some distance away the little boat was being bounced about on the waves by a frisky animal – only its tail could be seen.

21

The great wind bore furiously down from the pole onto the icy plateaus in the centre of the continent. It hit every surface, bringing the temperature way below freezing point and covering everything with a hard layer of ice. The icebreaker had picked up all the research groups and was now negotiating the Gerlach Canal, headed towards Bellingham base before leaving the continent. The storm had blown ice on the sea as well and the ship proceeded with difficulty. The freezing cold devoured everything; the life boats on the open bridge were a solid frozen sheet. Some of the equipment had remained there, including Miriam's tape recorder. From the covered deck Miriam and Felipe watched the sea whipped white by the gusts of wind.

"The proof is there, in the boat," she said.

"Let's go and see."

"You don't believe it? Old wives' tales, you say?"

"I didn't say that. Let's hear the tape."

"You'll have it as soon as I get it."

"Two biologists from Aurora Australis, the English base, have a similar sort of story to tell about a cetacean trying to tow a boat. But the boat got the worst of it, same as happened to you."

"I don't know what really went on. I'm still all mixed up."

"That's the only accurate data: confusion."

"The whale was confused too."

"The funny thing is that the whale can recognize a human so far away from the place where they met," said Felipe.

"They do strange things. It must be natural for them."

"Natural? Not likely!"

"But they're not aggressive and they are curious. It's natural for them to communicate with ease."

"Chatting in an ice cave with a pregnant whale – does that seem natural to you? You must have dreamt about it, I reckon."

They laughed. The ship drifted noisily on its stabilizers as the wind hurled an icy blast at the windows, fusing splashes of snow. A contorted image formed.

"See," said Miriam pointing to the glass. "There was something like that in the designs in the cave. Only that the mother was in front of them."

"You told me," Felipe concluded hurriedly. "Just a chance happening."

"It's something that happens very rarely. It seems water reacts that way, under certain conditions."

"Something like the little blocks of iceberg we put in the whisky," said Felipe. "They make an odd fizzing sound then mumble. If you pick up the sound with an amplifier, who knows what strange sort of utterances you end up with!"

He laughed and went back to the table where he was working on some data. Miriam remained where she was, her hooded head leaning against the glass. The ship pitched and swayed; the deck looked like a scene from a fairy tale; the lifeboat, a frozen flower with an oval shaped corolla. Two sailors stood on the covered deck checking the route. The low pressure engines gave out a laboured beat. In front of the bow a group of penguins circled around a spot. A dolphin surfaced and joined the circle. A bank of krill was coming to the surface and the circle filled with birds suddenly appearing from nowhere. Life exploded in the wind. The ship passed a row of tabular icebergs swept by the storm that were sending up white clouds of powdery ice.

"Perhaps we can take some photos," Miriam murmured to herself.

"Photos like these," said a voice behind her.

It was Antonina, the Russian biologist who worked with Miriam. She had followed everything from the ship. She handed Miriam a set of photographs: cetaceans, shapes drawn by the sea. In each of the photos the whales were trying to reach a body of ice, to hit it gently and carve out a platform in order to climb on it.

"I took them on an occasion similar to yours. I told you about it. I couldn't remember where they were but

I've found them at last. If you look closely you can see they are all females. See the fins?"

"Old wives' tales, they'd say." Miriam winked in the direction of Felipe and the two sailors. "Better not talk too much about it. They'd say we were mad."

"Yes, better not. But the tape recorder that you used to record everything – did you leave it out there?"

"Yes, in the boat, as soon as they pulled us up. It was windy and we made it back to the ship with great difficulty. I'll go and get it as soon as I can."

She pointed to the lifeboat in the bow that looked like a frozen walrus with huge white drooping whiskers.

"You'll have to wait a few days," said the biologist.

The ship's frame groaned. The vertical wind blew yet harder. It was the dominating element in these parts, leaving lines etched in the landscape and digging out valleys year after year.

The Russian woman went to the jug. She was a heavy-set woman with a square face and slit eyes. She made a cup of coffee, handed it to Miriam and sat down to talk. She spoke about phenomena connected with temperature, the limits of endurance of a mammal, communication between pregnant animals and finished by stating that even between females of different species communication is difficult in that condition.

"At Sakaman Lagoon they call it the telephone of the nest," Miriam replied.

"What do the males say?" asked the Russian woman pointing to the men.

"The usual stuff! No sense talking about it."

"Not even to Felipe?"

"He makes fun of the whole thing. But he's really excited about it."

"I know he's the type who can get worked up over anything. We have to keep him on our side."

"Forget it. He seems receptive, like a lot of the scientists here, but he'll only go so far."

"Well, do you want to shut them all out?"

"They only put up with me because they need my skill in statistical calculations. It's always been an ambiguous aspect of my work. You should've seen what happened at Sri Lanka – they almost packed me off to the loony bin for good."

She stopped talking. The wind had turned and was changing the patterns on the glass in front of the helmsman.

"You've got to try and convince them," said the Russian woman.

"I've got to come up with an angle that appeals to them, a set of data that is acceptable, that meets the standard."

The Russian woman got up, stretched, went to the window.

"Look, the aurora australis."

Giant brush strokes had painted the night sky above in blue and yellow. The bands of colour moved in an extinguished world that reflected the colours like strips of luminous water. Miriam went to look; the scene reminded her of the frozen lake and the meeting with the mother. The discharge was creating something out of nothing. She felt the aurora bearing down on her and ran stumbling towards Felipe, a feeling of love arising in her for each of the elements: the night, the sea, Felipe, the wind, the colours moving in the east – a carousel that involved them all, even the aurora australis that banished the dark from the night, like the krill banished hunger by giving itself up in the communion of the sea.

She listened in the great silence, then turned towards her companions. They were standing there, motionless, their eyes fixed on the lights dancing in the sky. The ship travelled on with a dull beat. The wind grew stronger. Miriam rubbed her ears; she wanted to be sure of what she was hearing. Gusts of wind etched new and surprising patterns on the glass that were rubbed out and replaced by yet different ones. They reminded her of sophisticated abstract art, similar to the patterns woven by the whale in the ice cave, as though they were the most ancient form of sea art. Excitement seized her by the throat, and to calm down she opened the door and went out. The wind dropped momentarily so she decided to go to the lifeboat to retrieve the tape recorder and ventured out onto the ice-covered deck on all fours. The snow seemed motionless. She advanced ten metres or so, then the bitterly cold wind returned and it was a struggle to go forward; she fought the air. Grabbing a succession of handholds, she managed to reach the bulkhead of the lifeboat, untied a corner of the tarpaulin and slipped in. As the colours of the aurora australis zigzagged in snake-like frenzy across the sky above, Miriam began searching for the tape recorder, rummaging through all sorts of tools: harpoons, bags, pumps, covered engines. Finally, she reached a corner where she could shelter from the cold under a pile of blankets, found the tape recorder, opened it and placed it on her breast to warm it. After a few minutes she put on the earphones and pressed the buttons. The machine sprang to life and she searched for the recording made at the ice lake. A human figure joined her. It was a sailor who had come to secure the moorings of the lifeboats. They tied down the tarpaulin that was flapping in the violent wind and sat near to each other. Miriam wanted him to listen to the recording while they waited for the wind to die down so as they could go back. She wanted someone else's opinion immediately so as not to remain alone with her fantasies. The tape played on, recalling the mother, the words she had heard. The sailor smiled in the semi-darkness, a gold tooth flashing in his mouth under grey eyes. They exchanged a few words as lightning flashed in the sky. The woman asked him if he understood and he nodded affirmatively. Then the wind grew stronger and the man tightened the ropes that held down the tarpaulin. The waves were sweeping the deck and it was dangerous to cross it. On long journeys the lifeboats were secured under steel covers. They waited, sitting close together for mutual warmth.

The sailor said a few words, pointing to the sky, to the aurora australis. He spoke, grinning, pointing to the tape recorder. Miriam's intuition told her that he knew something. They attempted to converse in a stammered sort of language. The man referred to the whales as though they were creatures from another world. Using his hands to make himself understood, he added that all limits, all boundaries, became different at this time and in this place – the female cetaceans felt it, communicating with each other in a unique manner.

The sailor held Miriam's hands so as to make her understand more easily, saying that he had been in a similar place with a biologist from his country who had gone through the same experience. Miriam asked if it was the woman with them on the ship but the man shook his head. It had happened during another journey. He then said something the woman did not understand but which made her feel uneasy, as though she were naked in front of a stranger. In that instant the tape recorder stopped. The sailor tried to get it working again, warming it against his body, but the cold had made it seize up. They sat there, talking as best they could. The man behaved in a child-like fashion, then assumed authoritarian tones, speaking forcefully, then tailed off with a quiet smile. Miriam was tense; the man was saying that originally all beings are female and that masculinity came later, an added extra as a transformation extending towards an infinite individuality. At least that was what Miriam thought she understood. Then he went on to say that the concept had been elaborated by scientists in his country. Using the dual language of words and gestures he explained that the planet on which they lived was a world of water and solitude where fire gave heat for an instant and that was when life came into being. But it was only for an instant, otherwise everything would be destroyed; there could not be too much fire, he said, or all would melt. The woman asked him to explain, but the sailor was not able to express himself more clearly and repeated in a sing-song tone of voice what he had already said twice, but she was not able to follow him. Outside the wind surged strongly, beating down violently on the lifeboat. Miriam moved even closer to the sailor who helped her to regain composure. She clung to him, trembling, to chase away the cold. The man turned her towards him, hugging her and she felt she was being sucked inside. She looked through a slit in the tarpaulin and saw the aurora australis change into light-filled narrow patterns. She felt the sailor embrace her, gently, protectively, and thought that every maternity began obscurely in this manner. The man's tongue felt hot, a taste of bitter almonds, blending with the surging of the body. She tried to break loose, felt the gold in his mouth, then breath turned to heat, overcame her, and the two bodies become one pulsating skin. All resistance vanished. The colours of the sky entered through the slits of the sheltering tarpaulin; the rest was darkness. Miriam heard the whistling sound return; a strange man was embracing her, as had happened to the mother in the ocean. But it was not possible that this was the only value chosen by nature for the reproduction of life. She tried to free herself, bit the man, pushed him away, fell down. She felt her dress being torn off with the same haste of another male that had enchanted her in the tropics, on the warm sea.

She lay under the aurora that was slicing the sky, shaken by the shadow that held her tight. She felt as though she were part of that aurora, a hot, senseless, point of union that her womb would accept or reject automatically, after that irresistible moment. She looked up. The lights in the sky had all suddenly come on, and the cold wind was biting her. Then darkness hit her heavily.

An unexpected shadow suddenly blotted out everything, throwing itself on them. Miriam huddled up as best she could while the sailor fought the shape that had appeared and was trying to tear him apart. Miriam felt the bite of the wind increase; half the lifeboat was uncovered and the wind warped her in icy coldness. A cramp blocked her belly. Two figures were outlined under the streaked light of the aurora, locked together in a primeval battle that annihilated her. Slowly, as she cowered in a corner, a savage female expectation returned. The two contenders were striking at each other, their groans a measure of the violence of their blows. As the struggle intensified, they ended up on the bottom of the lifeboat. One of the two twitched, then lay still. The other picked up an object. The tape recorder began playing again, and for an instant the recording made at the lake could be heard: " . . . You've come . . . the patterns . . . one over the other . . ."

The voice died down as the man on the bottom of the boat hit the other. The machine flew out onto the deck, on the icy floor, and slid away with the pitching of the ship. Miriam yelled. The sailor jumped out, tried to catch the machine while holding on with the other hand. The tape recorder disappeared over the ship's side and the sailor headed for the door through which he had come out on deck.

Miriam struggled to lift herself by the elbows. The full force of the wind hit her. In front of her was Felipe's face, dripping with sweat, and red with blood or the krill blown about by the wind.

Miriam was gasping for breath; her work had vanished in the sea. The cold was everywhere and she craved for warmth. She reached out to Felipe's face, licked the blood off with her tongue and dragged him down into the boat. She felt for his tongue, his dazzling white teeth, and squeezed his hard tongue. The strips of light in the sky had become wider, brighter. She gave out a cry and lost her senses, clinging to the man.

Outside, the lifeboat had become once more a vessel of ice, at the end of the night, as the waves rolled in the dark of the sea.

22

The Antarctic convergence is a cross-roads of the sea at 50° latitude south. The warm waters from the north meet up with and slide over the icy waters from the south. The whales from the Indian Ocean pass through here on the way to their feeding fields in the far south. Months later they cross the convergence again on their way back. On the track of a river of krill, the mother crossed the Antarctic convergence to the north east of Heard Island, drifting with the currents. It was her usual route along the sea pastures. The whales followed paths that, over large expanses of sea, did not coincide with the routes taken by other marine travellers.

On the borders of the icy ocean the krill gave out a weak phosphorescence that barely managed to reveal a landscape without bottom or surface. It is an area which harbours considerable biological energy in tremendous maelstroms that give primitive force back to the sea. Life forms are sucked in or pushed out in shallow areas, according to the energy they produce. The krill and other minute organisms return to the frozen south. Others, like the sharks, go back north. Only the warm-blooded animals – penguins, seals, whales and killer-whales – can cross the line of convergence. It is a hard experience for the larger animals who would rather be far away, near more peaceful coasts or inlets. Here they sometimes search for the paths initially followed by their progenitors. This is what attracted the mother.

The baby was growing in her womb. The change of temperature on the surface caused the expansion of the internal organs. She felt they had become heavier as the sea exposed her to flashes of sunlight that coloured her blue amidst the blue water. Southwards sheets of ice melted among fluctuating clouds of krill. The ocean swallowed up the crustaceans glazed by the force of the water. Sun and ice confronted each other.

The mother emerged in front of a lump of ice, residue of Antarctic bulwarks. Transparent and shiny, it displayed a scene frozen in time: a whale, its mouth still open, had been frozen in there during a migration long ago. Its open eyes shone in the iceberg. The lashing tail was held still and a line of bubbles came out of its mouth representing the last breath. Perhaps the hibernation had conserved a tiny spark of life deep down. The mother felt past and present coming together in the block of ice that preserved her ancient comrade. The slabs of ice were covered by a huge flock of birds. All around fish and seals scurried away. The whale passed in front of the floating iceberg. In the ice she could clearly see that frozen figure, then she saw some killer-whales also prisoners in the block. The mother ran to help her companion, ramming the ice, sending up dazzling splinters.

Inspired by that strange desire that at other times, in other places, led her to attempt to free stranded companions, the mother went on ramming the iceberg as it spun slowly but the only result of her efforts were deep scratches on her skin and on the underlying fat. A gap opened up in the white mass and part of the iceberg dropped away. The mother avoided the obstacle and retreated. Regenerated by the polar voyage, she felt the fat under her skin ready to withstand any trial. The pregnant belly pulsed. Something was calling her over the frequencies to which she was receptive. Perhaps it was a call from a beach where every now and then a whale ran aground. The vibration was refracted by the whale in the ice as in a prism that scrambles light and sensations. She sensed the suffering of the other and recalled the torments of her last child, savaged by the killer-whales. The whale in the ice, too, had been attacked by the killer whales who had also been frozen. Perhaps she could help it. She began ramming the iceberg again and snapped off a corner. The crack widened; the iceberg rocked trying to find a new equilibrium. The mother felt the water of life pour out as had happened in the white lake. She hit the iceberg expecting the immobile cetacean to slide into the water. All around the dual temperatures of the swirling waters separated dissimilar types: minute fauna to the south, large fauna to the north. The mother dived alongside the iceberg that went a few hundred metres down into the water. Strange languages became clear for brief moments. She understood the attack of the enemies, their vitality. In her heart she felt the shout of the frozen killer-whales; they did not represent a danger. She returned to attack the ice with renewed energy, her adrenalin turned, focusing on a forgotten impulse. The mother considered that every warm-blooded creature belonged to a single species. Heat against the cold that had to be conquered and destroyed. She surfaced to blow. A herd of cetaceans approached her; little black whales. They too, like her blue companions, travelled over all the seas and called to other over enormous distances, but they did not have the power of the blue whales. The black whales travelled on and the mother remained alone, resting in the warm waves that slowly but surely conquered the cold waters of the south. She was now well into the convergence zone, all-enclosing in its convulsions almost as though another sea were being born. In the ocean everything emptied out and filled up again. The mother had experienced the same upheaval every time she had given birth.

It was a passionate, fluid stimulus that drew her in every direction. The pressure of the sea thrust her up and she surfaced in the sunlight. The krill had gone and a shoal of dolphins was rapidly drawing away. The mother searched for the whale set in the ice but there was nothing around. She went down in an impetuous dive, an outburst which made her feel every creature was a little one in need of help. She engaged in a half-conscious search for her mother, the one who had one day carried her in her womb. She wanted to seek out her origin and suddenly her mother appeared.

She was infinitely larger, the face coloured a deeper blue than hers, the tail stronger in striking and the eyes lost amidst a thousand bubbles of oxygen. She saw her mother's birth pangs, felt herself being born, turned over, fed and cradled. The icebergs had been left behind like the shadows of ancestors. To the north was the outline of the blue path that led the cetaceans towards the warmth of the sun. She swam towards it as her lungs emptied out in gusts of vapour.

All was present. Her mother was there, giving birth to her again as happened every season when she passed through the area. She tried to make herself as small as possible in order to allow herself to be cradled. Waves and currents, whirlpools and caresses of warm water passed over her, lifting her up towards the air, then plunging her down into the depths.

The sea was her mother and the flux that made her move were its caresses.

The iceberg was in front of her once more; the shoal of killer-sharks was there, frozen in the ice.

The mother recognized her traditional enemies, feeling the freezing cold, that strange alternative of suspended life. She looked for air bubbles with the skill of air-breathing animals when they submerge in the sea. They carried an interrupted message that came out of their sharp teeth flashing in the ice; a fatal sign for animals of her species, but she recognized their importance. She went up, following the iceberg whose peak shone in the sun. Fear and fury returned, etched into that transparent mountain, among the outlines of the fibres imprisoned in immobile rays alternating with streaks of blood that awakened a memory.

It had been a day of the hunt, further to the south. The whale was wounded and attracted a shoal of killer-whales. Icebergs towered all around and the battle waged amidst them. The catabatic wind, the vertical wind from the pole, had borne down, crushing hunter and hunted in its icy grip. The storm raged on, the sea became tinted with blood and the sky filled with cries. All became enclosed.

The ice swallowed up the scene under the continually falling sleet and the event froze to a halt, for years, for ever. Other layers of ice condensed and fused together, then they broke apart, floating half-submerged towards the Antarctic convergence, melting as they progressed in their journey. Now the scene was being displayed for the last time before disappearing into the sea.

As the mother observed the protagonists of that drama, a shoal of live killer-whales rushed towards her and the frozen scene sprang to life. The whale fled, diving deep down where her hunters could not follow. She swam for a long time, then surfaced, passing her days in solitary dives, until she perceived the call of her species, a distant song. She had entered that ocean without losing herself, in a well-defined network that the whales soaked up like perfume and the mother followed its trial.

Something was calling her. The pressure strengthened the impulse and the whale, like a blue star, began to climb towards the sun that was descending into the horizon. The call was leading her towards the east where night was falling. It had left the rhythm of life on the warm coasts and had now been picked up by the heartbeats in this faraway pulse of energy. It blew over the water and the stamen rose, dissipating, the rippled ocean an empty expanse. The mother felt she was alone, ready willing and able like an athlete in a stadium all to himself. There was nothing around her, only that invocation, that string of sounds, perturbed her. Killer-whales, embryo, clashes, icebergs, sea-horses of the land danced in her memory.

The sun cut the waves casting long shadows before plunging into the sea. Hundreds of miles in front of her was the land. The call came from there. She swam on with equal rhythm for hours, then for days. The call for help penetrated her body, right through to the lumpy package swelling her belly that would one day ripen and fall out, taking with it all other invocations.

She vaguely remembered that the female sea-horses of the land who lived on a warm island felt the same excitement too. The call became scrambled, grew in intensity. It came from a place on the sea shore. The mother increased her strokes. A sort of killer-whale brushed past her. It was a docile black whale, smaller than the others of the species that transmitted the call. As the animal vanished, swimming towards the invisible coast, the ocean became silent once more, a bank of jellyfish drifting across the expanse. Then came the night.

The arena was empty again, but great encounters could begin at any moment in the dark.

23

The Antarctic convergence had been left behind in the south with its birds, its icebergs and its whirlpools. The whale felt the temperature changing. The layers of fat under her skin protected her. Other animals appeared, shoals of fish that came out of the pelagic larder whose doors had opened for an instant. The body of the great mammal picked up a new pulse that took her towards the blue breach where a multitude of sundry organisms were ready to attack or to flee. They were thick-set gaudily-coloured creatures, forms forgotten by the evolutionary process in the middle of the sea. Bold or fearful, they attacked or fled from the whale, milling around without letting her touch them. It was a long sea, waves crisscrossing, sudden gusts of spray, a misty field under a leaden sky.

The whale followed the call that came from a group of cetaceans concentrated around a faraway beach. She followed the line of this invocation over the waves.

Killer-whales came and went. The sea took on a deep blue colour, then plunged into grey streaked with clouds.

The wind was blowing in the same direction. A group of humpback whales appeared, white-finned leaping cetaceans. The killer-whales came up again, leaping in the bubbling water.

The whales were under attack in a flurry of bites and lashing tails as the battle dragged on for days with lengthy pauses.

One morning the animals reached the coast. Leaping high out of the water, the humpback whales could see land. After millions of waves the landscape settled in a crown of hills.

In front the beach extended as far as the eye could see. Round waves rolled between sky and sea. The killer-whales left the humpbacks and rushed after a huge shoal of herring. It was an orgy and the humpbacks joined in the banquet but they soon headed out to sea again, marking their path with silvery leaps. The killer-whales were drunk with food and started playing, chasing each other along the coastline, on the crest of the waves that broke there. Then they disappeared all together and their place was taken by a similar type of fish, slightly smaller but without the white colouring on the chest. They were black whales with globe-shaped heads, blackfish attracted by a call, the same one that had guided the mother for days. One of the cetaceans began to run on the crest of a wave that broke, then wriggled vigourously to return to safer waters. At the same time it was searching for the companion that had transmitted the call. Other black whales followed its example acting like patrol boats in a game that brought them closer to the beach as they tumbled and bounced. On the shallow bottom a female saw one of her kind who was stranded. It rushed to its aid, followed by other whales who formed a daisy pattern around the animal stuck on a sand bank. An instant later the rescuers were caught in a trap.

The whole shoal, about sixty whales, floundered about in the shallow water. Some managed to float free but came back to form the daisy so as to help the others and the trap sprung again. The sun was approaching its zenith among a few whisps of cloud.

The event soon involved the whole community as other whales, that had come in answer to the call, were caught in the trap. The bay was alive with animals.

The hours ticked away. Men appeared on the surrounding hills and many of them came down into the water to reach the trapped whales, forming other types of daisy patterns in an attempt to set them free. They began to drag the whales with ropes or to push them with tractors fitted with wheels for travelling on the sand, in the low tide. The bay filled up from one headland that marked its boundaries to the other. When the sun set, hundreds of people crowded together, black spots beside hundreds of whales, between beach and waves.

The men pushed the cetaceans towards the open sea, but the whales returned to the land. It was a sight never seen before as men threw the catch into the sea and the catch persisted in coming back. And so it went on, as the tractor headlights bore through the night in all directions.

The operation was interrupted, then picked up again in the morning, at sunrise, when the tractors went back to work lifting the stranded whales which were loaded onto trucks and carried to the far end of the bay where they were launched into the sea from the headland. Some headed out, others swam back into the trap. It was a nightmarish, yet enchanting scene.

The men drenched the dry skin of the whales with water or covered it with wet cloths. The cetaceans could not stand dehydration and in increasingly greater numbers passively submitted to whatever happened to them. With one accord, the whole population of the costal village on the other side of the bay set aside all other activities and came out on the beach.

It was a community on the south west tip of the Australian continent. Men, women and children came down to the beach, working in an orderly and disciplined way, as in an emergency.

The second night fell as the work went on under motionless stars. On the nearest hills a row of vehicles with headlights turned on completed the scene among loudspeakers and field kitchens. A few whales headed for the open sea to the applause of the humans.

The rising of the sun brought back light and the colours of dawn.

Beyond the waters of the bay, the sun shone on a blue whale. She had followed the call but her auditory system had also picked up something else. She approached the headland where the black whales were being thrown into the sea by an unknown monster.

The whale listened to the sounds that followed their first splash amidst the waves. Acutely aware of the presence of the sea-horses of the land, she drew near to the cliff from where the other whales had been thrown into the sea and entered a tidal canal.

In her belly she felt the creature about to be born, the sun concealed in her blood, a new day dawning inside her. All that was happening around her became labour pains.

The mother blew. She had seen the humpbacks go back into the sea from the cliff. They fell with a sharp splash pouring out of the hard yellow muzzle of a terrestrial animal with an amazingly horrendous mouth. So now the largest animal mouth no longer belonged to the cetaceans: a new era was dawning. Perhaps the blue whales had reached the end of their era. The monster huffed again. Who knows if the the sea-horses of the land listened to its sound? The baby jerked in her belly as the mother retreated towards the open sea, then headed back towards the headland. She was searching for the female sea-horse of the land she knew and she felt was nearby. A few black whales passed her; she called out to them but they drew away sending out confused signals she could not understand. The blue whale transmitted other sounds. She picked up the sounds of sea-horses of the land not far away, on the beach.

The sea-horses of the land were odd creatures. They migrated like the birds from one place to the other, reappearing on new beaches, from the frozen wastes to the torrid tropics. They migrated just like the whales and were now trying to form a daisy. Now was the time to approach them. She drew closer to the cliff where the monster arched its spine to hurl the beached whales into the sea. From there she would try to call the female sea-horse.

She listened to the sound of the monster that kept on spitting out whales. It was always the same ones that kept coming back to run aground. Time moved in a circular motion like the dance above the volcanos of the depths or on the white lake. She blew and a jet of vapour dissipated high in the air.

The abilities to absorb and communicate blended in her brain, almost as if a barrier between land and sea were being eliminated. She began to splash around the headland with her tail. Something replied from the beach. The sea-horses of the land wanted to make contact, but they continued to push the whales back into the sea. Unknown constants penetrated the fog that for millennia had blocked access to the brains of different species. The whale felt the other female was also expecting and sent out her call, then repeated it. Mimic, essential for communicating, had become sound.

Transmitting faint whistling sounds, she approached the beach. Perhaps the female sea-horse would pick up the signal. Otherwise the language seemed an uncertain echo.

The cetacean spun round in a circle in an attempt to participate in what was happening. She waited, transmitting signals that were not picked up. Nearby, crowds of black creatures emerged from the sea to meet with the sea-horses of the land and were pushed back into the water. The cetaceans were seeking their past, the sea-horses their future. They met for an instant and drew apart immediately, like the gears of a ruthless machine. The great whale felt it, like a spasm that unnerved her. She attempted to go forward, hoping that the female sea-horse would reply, and a wave dragged her onto the sandy floor.

Now there was danger. She called out for help but no one replied. Everyone was concentrating on the black whales. All alone, not far from the cliff where the other whales were dropping into the sea, the mother repeated her cry for help, a faint hiss.

On the land, Miriam heard the whistle. It had been happening to her with increasing regularity since she had returned home pregnant.

When the news about the massive beachings had spread, Miriam had rushed to the spot with the other scientists of her group. Because of her experience she had been invited to take part in the operation which held the whole continent in suspense. For three days the work progressed marked by successes and setbacks. The woman did not go into the water because of her condition, but took observations and advised on how to communicate with the whales. The rescuers had to talk to the whales as they pushed them out to sea and wet them, imitating their sounds. The whales were small, about six metres long, and they attempted to move on their own. They needed to be encouraged, touched on the sides, never on the head or they would have trouble breathing. They sometimes opened their mouths but were not dangerous. The humans could gently take hold of their fins, steering them out to sea and away from the land which they kept trying to reach. As soon as they were able to swim again they had to be pushed like tame bulls. Sometimes it worked, sometimes it didn't. Some of the whales died on the shore; others swam away.

For hours hundreds and hundreds of people came and went from the water, while vehicles provided a shuttle service to the village.

Miriam sat on the beach next to a table. A woman who was making coffee handed a piping hot cup to a boy just come out dripping from the water. It was an afternoon flooded with sunlight. Miriam drank some coffee too; then, amidst the shouts and the noise from the loudspeakers, she heard the whistling sound and looked out to sea. A tractor churned by holding a whale in its shovel like a mother carrying a young one in its jaws. Miriam turned round.

Further to the north, the blue whale also turned in the water. She was trapped by a sand bank and spent long lapses without moving. Then she rolled on her side causing the water to swirl. Nobody saw her. Again she transmitted her call, pushing the sand with her tail, but was unable to roll over. The baby was thrashing about in her belly. Night fell on her attempts to free herself.

Daybreak found many whales still stranded on the beach. Others had left. About twenty hadn't made it. A group of men in blue and red overalls was pushing the whales back into the water. They had reached the limit of enudurance. Miriam watched as women and children came and went. Out at sea the fins of the liberated cetaceans were like a row of little boats outlined against the sunlight on the flat ocean.

24

Stuck on the sand bank that held her prisoner the whale sensed that everyone was going away, even the other female. She had searched for the woman and had felt her searching in the same way. But now there was more, something between a mother and a child who feels but does not understand. The beaching had accelerated the critical period of the birth process. She sent out the call of her species but there was no reply; she was all alone. Her heart beat more rapidly and her fins flapped, a communication between body tissues beyond instinct in a situation where instinct had become obscured.

Her back was exposed to the sun and the whale wet it by flapping tail and fins to throw up the salty liquid that was so vital for her. She felt a contraction in her belly; the baby was moving. Birth pains shook her as violent contractions made her roll on one side, then on the other. She was held in a vice, torn by the scorching air above, by the friction of the sand bank below. Inside the baby fought to come out and the mother felt like a bunch of seaweed tossed about in a storm. Deep in her womb a vortex sprung up banishing all desire to help all other creatures. Everything was upside down and she became again the primeval mother as nature overwhelmed her with the most ancient tribulation in the world.

In that vortex she heard the cries of the whales on the beach.

Empty whales passed by, blue ones, black ones, even those who never showed themselves on the coast, the deep sea mesoplodents, wrecks of cetaceans from the mists of antiquity. It was the world of the mother, returning like an instinct determined to survive.

The sea-horses of the land were attempting to save

the other whales, but were not helping her. They followed mysterious laws that defied instinct. The mother had tried to reach the shore to establish a new link between land and sea, to help whoever needed it, whether whale or sea-horse. But she had lost the way; the sand bank held her and she could not free herself by using her tail and fins. She sent out the call for help. The sound went way out and reached another female. On the beach the black humpbacks heard it, but they were upset, confused and could not get their bearings. The sea-horses of the land lifted the marine bodies, pushing them towards the sea with their brutal passion. The eyes of the floating whale could only make out the broken line that separated land from water. Now it was up to the mother to help herself and the little one about to be born.

The pains stopped and she sent out the call for help again. She was almost entirely underwater, but her belly was still in the grip of the sand bank, and she was stuck. She rolled over as best she could, putting her weight on the mass of fat that enveloped her and absorbed lacerations and lashings. Her heartbeats increased convulsively. With all her energy she resisted the thrust of the baby, of the sand bank and of the long waves that pushed her towards the rocks at the base of the cliff. Everything was trying to pin her down, inside and outside. All she had left to save herself was her heart and her tail. She also flexed her fins but they were weak like the wings of a butterfly over the sea.

The sand underneath held her fast. The water around frothed with her efforts to free herself, dragging her towards the nearby cliff. The fear of the rocks made her lash out with her tail, opening new gaps in the sand bank and piling up more sand underneath, compressing her belly where the creature was pushing from the inside to get out. She listened attentively in the direction of the land, seeking help. Whales were no longer falling from the cliff; the enormous yellow mouth had disappeared. On the shore of the bay the sea-horses of the land were quietening down, preparing to leave the beach. The mother was alone. The long waves that crashed on the rocks freed her for an instant from the grip of the sand only to thrust her back into it. Another whale of her kind was swimming nearby; she called out to it and received a reply. They made contact.

On the beach a female sea-horse heard it and turned around. She looked towards the headland and noticed a huge yellowish block outlined against the light drawing away. In the bay the waves hid an enormous blue-coloured belly that was opening by the reef. A tail flashed in the air. The undertow obscured the event, dragging it back. Under the tail flailing in the air a body slipped out, the oblong head coming last. A wave crashed in and dispersed the scene, throwing two flashing unequal tails against the rocks that were dragged away with the retreating water. The birth had made the whale lighter, setting her free from the sand bank.

She picked herself up with a groan, blood and foam pouring from her, then everything disappeared. An enormous blue female came from the ocean, searching for the abandoned body, supported it and pushed the baby out to sea. The three whales swam away leaving a trail of cloudy humours. On the beach all noise had ceased. The only sound was the undertow created by the waves. The red streaks in the sky were like comet trails.

The two blue whales headed out to sea; between them bounded a rose-tinted ball.

The mother was exhausted and allowed her companion to guide her. The little one was already sucking milk. The whale that had come to help had lost its child to the killer whales and had now found another one. History was repeating itself. They swam until dawn, lulled by the ocean waves.

The new whale suckled the little one too. Towards evening they all sank into lethargy, half of their brain dreaming, the other half vigilant. Although half asleep they cradled the baby, rocking it with their huge tails. The beach was empty. The tractor tracks on the sand looked like trails left by huge beasts that had come out of the sea and disappeared behind the hills.

The mother blew, then let out a high-pitched whistle. Conversation with the female sea-horse was dwingling, mingled with the messages exchanged between the two whales swimming side by side. Time had become cyclic, the usual pattern for the whales, as the great creatures travelled away with the baby, and the attempt to communicate with another being flowed back within the barriers between the species. Only a whistling sound remained, the whisper of a conversation just begun, increasingly vague and already dissipating under the sky. Perhaps it would rise again one day, like the daisy pattern of a new season.

The whales were floating in the calm bay where other cetaceans gathered in spring to give birth, their huge bulks diaphanous in the darkening blue. The baby blew and swam slantwise between the enormous swinging tails that rocked it, ready to protect it against any killer whales that might appear.

Two huge columns of vapour followed by a whistling sound went up before the whales disappeared.

On land a pregnant woman jumped up and ran towards the nearby headland. On the way she saw the last of the tractors returning with happy little flags tied high up on the exhaust pipes. They were going back to the farms scattered around the countryside and were blowing their horns like a comic naval squadron. The whales that had been set free were far out at sea.

"What weird animals! What the hell's biting them to make them rush aground like that?" shouted one of the drivers as he drove past Miriam.

Miriam wanted to reply, but the tractor was making too much noise so she just waved. Someone grabbed her arm; it was Kitzy, the friend she was staying with.

"There's nothing more to do here," she said. "Come in."

"There's another one down there," replied Miriam.

The other argued, dragging her away, but Miriam broke free and told her the story once more.

"Your blue whale! But the ones that came here are black!"

"I sense its call. I'm sure. I feel I'm missing a meeting that's important to me, that I've been expecting for a long time. Let me go. I've got to get down there."

"But it's all finished and we're exhausted with all that's happened down there on the beach."

"I've got to look for her. I must go."

"But what are you looking for? A whale in the middle of the sea? There's not even a boat around."

"Let me go, please."

"But you have to think of the baby."

"I've got to go."

"Take it easy. Let's sit down for a bit."

Kitzy sat down on a bench, pulled out a packet of cigarettes and offered Miriam one. She was strong, middle-aged, blond hair tied in a bun. Miriam took a cigarette; her hands were trembling and she inhaled angrily as time marched on and her anxiety grew. She wanted to react, but was unable to move. The whistling sound in her ear kept rising and falling, then grew weaker as the low tide exposed the empty beach. Miriam went on smoking; she was in a daze, unable to do anything else as the sound kept fluctuating in intensity. It seemed a farewell. The sea grew small, hostile under the dying sun. Miriam saw it as a prison of sky and water that released someone's faint call. An invisible wall had now returned excluding her from the blue water beneath her. Her heartbeats echoed like those of the mother in the ice cave. She wanted to run, search for the whale, but remained there motionless. Her condition, the coming of night, the words of her friend, held her back. Only the whistling sound pushed her on, painfully. Men had helped the black whales come to the land to meet them; they had pushed them back into the sea to save them and the cetaceans had gone away. Some of the whales had returned to die, compelled by a mysterious instinctive force that seemed collective folly. But Miriam was mindful of an additional achievement; the hissing sound was an appointment, a deep all-involving message that told her with absolute certainty her whale was near. But where was she?

The cigarette was almost out and the smoke made her eyes smart. Kitzy kept insisting that they go back inside. Miriam was expecting; maybe the whale too, was her silent thought. All of her story was true. She was certain of this, even though her colleagues would always treat her with skeptical condescension. It was a window on a world of unfathomable mysteries and inscrutable patterns that involved her. But each of the two females had to follow through in her own time, one on land, the other in the sea. Miriam put out her cigarette.

"You know, that hissing sound in the ear I was telling you about," she began.

"You hear too many voices!" replied the other, getting up. "Come in. I'll make you a coffee."

The last ray of the yolk-red sun scattered behind the

clouds. The reflection flooded in red the headland and the waves breaking against it. A man threw something into the water from the observation post. Far out, a pink ball leapt for an instant from the ocean. The two women watched until their eyes filled with flashes. Miriam looked down; from the butt she had discarded, a thin wisp of bluish smoke was rising in oblong form, followed by a smaller one that merged with the first: two creatures clasped in the arms of fantasy. Miriam watched the figures disperse in the air. The whistling sound had also dispersed; she felt her heart stop for an instant. Kitzy started to walk back home; Miriam followed.

"I'm sleepy," said Miriam throwing herself on the bed in the front room, next to a green partition. But her eyes did not close; in her pupils were the images of the paths of infinity where all the different creatures came into momentary contact. For an instant she had penetrated a secret world where the eyes of many animals shone like a huge constellation. A fox terrier slipped in through the door and came up to sniff at the woman on the bed.

"Down Foxy," said Kitzy from the other room. "Leave Miriam be. She's on a trip in the dream world. She has a date."

The dog and the woman went into the other room where she prepared some dog food and took it outside, followed by Foxy. The sea had already changed colour. The cetaceans floated in their dream world; the little whale's dreams were chaotic, the larger one was dreaming of a realistic story with the odd patch of colour. It was the story of two beings who had already met: the great whale was calling the female sea-horse who slid into the sea and swam towards her. The female sea-horse found support on the head of the other, slipping over it like a weightless shadow and holding on to the tiny animals that had always lived there. She had tried to tear them off once, but there was room for all on the head of the immense animal whose skin was the same colour as the ocean it swam in.

The shadow on top of her head slipped over her short-sighted eye bringing on a strange sort of fear. The fear vanished as the huge body became transparent and the whisper faded away. Then for the first time she heard the sea-horse of the land sing a sweet and gentle song that spread throughout the blue water. It was a song without the harsh sounds that the sea-horses of the land usually uttered when they tried to speak to the whales and which caused absolute silence in the natural order. This, however, was a lullaby like the one the whale sometimes sang while rocking her baby. A shoal of silvery fish had also stopped to listen. Then a faint noise dispersed the song like a puff of wind that blows the petals off a flower.

Afterword

Gaetano Rando

The Blue Whale is Stanislao Nievo's fifth novel and marks an important and interesting development in the literary career of one of Italy's foremost contemporary authors.

Stanislao Nievo turned to creative writing after a varied, sometimes colourful, certainly brilliant career which has involved studies in marine biology, extensive world-wide travel, journalism, photography and the production of documentaries. Always deeply committed to conservation issues, his activities have ranged widely from founder member of Wwf Italia to the recent *parchi letterari* project undertaken for the publisher Editore Abete. The project involves the identification, both in Italy and other countries, of areas of literary importance, their official recognition as *literary parks* and the production of a book outlining the natural and social ambience of each park, as well as the life and works of the author associated with the area. It is a project of international significance and allows Nievo to combine his commitment to ecological issues with his wide cultural knowledge and his skills as a writer, as he has also done in *La Foresta di Tarvisio* (Rome: Autostrade Gruppo IRI, Italsat, 1986).

Nievo's creative writing has rapidly earned him a reputation as one of the most interesting and atypical authors of contemporary Italian fiction, an image encouraged by the complex, but substantially unitary structure of his narrative, his penchant for the exotic and the unusual (a rare element in Italian letters) and a tendency towards experimentalism. Critics have singled out in his works the quest for the origins of our existence in its various phases (Anon 1990), for the most intimate and most hidden mysteries of existence (Sgorlon 1990), a quest which is seen as the only antidote against the chaotic void of a tragic and discredited history-ridden world (Sgorlon 1990). One of the key elements in this quest is the sea, which is a predominating presence in three out of five novels, as well as in a number of short stories.

The element of the sea and stories set in faraway exotic places are two aspects of Nievo's fiction which make him stand apart from most contemporary Italian writers. Despite Italy's geographical location, its literature is markedly devoid of maritime themes, although there are the very rare exceptions to be found in the works of Emilio Salgari and Raffaello Brignetti. Mario Luzi, among other critics of Nievo's work, has pointed out that

> Stanislao Nievo has given Italian literature a dimension that, amazingly enough, was lacking in a country like ours with its peninsular shape whose history is peopled with famous navigators, as well as hardy and courageous land travellers. We do, of course, find maritime themes in Italian literary tradition, but only exclusively with reference to coastal waters and blue water sailors (Luzi 1990).

In real life too, Nievo, unlike Salgari, has been a "hardy and courageous" traveller over land and sea in a search for the hidden truths and the explanation of the mysteries of existence to be found in remote and faraway places (Topi 1990). No armchair novelist, he has travelled extensively in Europe, New Guinea and Australia in pursuit of materials for his fourth novel *Le Isole del paradiso* (1987), while his quest for *The Blue Whale* has led him from the warm waters of the Indian Ocean to the icy wastes of the Antarctic.

His first three novels, although set in Italy, nevertheless also involved travel and investigation both for the author and their protagonists. *Il Prato in fondo al mare* (1974) is based on the mysterious disappearance at sea of the ship carrying Stanislao's great-uncle, Ippolito Nievo, from Palermo to Naples in 1861, and is both an imaginative reconstruction of the shipwreck, as well as the forceful narration of the author's attempts to solve one of Italy's greatest maritime mysteries. In *Aurora* (1979) Alessandro is fascinated to the point of obsession by an obscure pre-Roman goddess Mater Matuta, a mysterious Mediterranean deity of Eastern origin who presided over the birth event, to the point of engaging in a search which involves the examination of old documents, visits to museums, interviews with archaeologists, a mystic experience during a nocturnal visit to the remains of her temple. An expedition below the modern-day city of Rome in search of the statue of an angel under the Palatine provides the starting point for Nievo's third novel *Il Palazzo del silenzio* (1985), whose protagonist becomes involved in an intricate attempt to fathom the legend of Mezio Curzio, the Roman knight who was reputed to have disappeared after jumping with his horse into an abyss which had opened up in the Roman Forum in order to save the city from threatened destruction.

The subversion of factuality and science transposed from the personal to the social sphere is an important element of Nievo's fourth novel *Le Isole del paradiso.* As in his previous works there is the contrast between nature and civilization, time and timelessness, the search for realities beyond the apparent. But it is also the first of Nievo's novels not to have an Italian setting. Comparisons could be made with other writers of adventure literature, especially Conrad, Melville, Stevenson and Salgari, although Nievo is very different compared to these literary precedents, *Le Isole del paradiso* being partly a historical novel, partly an adventure novel, fascinating for the poignancy in communicating the grandiose dream which inspired the attempt to found a colony in the southern seas. The first part of the novel is set in Melanesia in the 1880s and relates the ill-fated attempt to found the colony of Nouvelle France at Port Breton in New Ireland which brought to Australia the immigrants who were to found New Italy in Northern NSW. In a sense it is the prehistory of the first Italian rural settlement in Australia, and although only a few chapters are set in this country, Australia is an important thematic element in the novel. In the second part the author enters the novel as one of its characters as he traces the story of the events before, during and after the Port Breton settlement. It is a search which leads him to travel from Italy to Spain, France, Switzerland, Melanesia and Australia. He becomes in effect the last emigrant as he establishes a link across time with the original colonists.

If at one level the *Isole del paradiso* presents the quest for myth, the creation of myth and the discovery of the "lost" part of the tribe – leading to a mystical reunion across time and space, life and death, with the Fruilian migrants dispersed in New Ireland (Mattei 1990) – using the sea as the mechanical means of the voyage, *The Blue Whale* may be seen as the quest for common origins through the medium of the sea and confirms a shift of focus in the direction of Nievo's narrative. In his first three novels there is a concern with the investigation of and the search for myth; in the *Isole* and, particularly, *The Blue Whale,* the point of departure is the quest for the common origins of the world to which we belong.

A further element of continuity between the two novels is the discourse on nature as a dynamic, positive and vital element which contrasts with man's static negativism. Nature, personified in the blue whale, is seen as "enormous, extremely powerful, but docile and harmless" (Sgorlon 1990). In *The Blue Whale* there are also significant links with Nievo's earlier works: the search for a common archetypal mother figure embodied in the two protagonists, Miriam and the whale, can be seen as an extrapolation of the quest for the archetypal mother figure initiated in *Aurora,* while the ocean is described as an immense aquatic womb (see Benelli 1990:5) and provides a significant tie with *Il Prato in fondo al Mare.* However, despite these continuities, *The Blue Whale* presents a new direction in Nievo's writing: at one level the novel can be seen as a metaphor of the relationship between human language and the mysterious language of the whales, between science and literature; at yet another level there is a significant involvement in the exploration of ecological themes, a matter of long-standing concern to Nievo who, it will be recalled, is one of the founders of WWF Italia.

The main character of *The Blue Whale*, Miriam,[1] is a young Australian statistician employed by the National Aquatic System (NAS) as part of a research team engaged in the study of sounds emitted by whales. The team's working hypothesis is that these sounds are used by the whales as a means of communication not only among themselves but as an attempt to make contact with mankind, and the obvious comparison is made with dolphins who also manage to communicate with man in their own fashion. In the group of blue whales which are the subject of the project and which consider man to be a sort of terrestrial sea-horse there is one in particular, a large thirty-metre long female, which the team calls "the mother" because she affectionately tends a calf and displays a distinct partiality towards her terrestrial counterparts – the women members of the team. The initial part of the novel is presented in a style which very much suggests the description of a scientific research project. However, fable and myth are soon introduced in the narrative and become predominant elements. NAS has set up an observation centre in an old lighthouse on the west coast of Sri Lanka, an enchanted isle noted for *serendipity*. As the team continues its observations of the whales Miriam becomes increasingly fascinated by "the mother," who saves her when she is swept overboard and speaks to her as she lies in a trance-like state. As a result of this experience Miriam actively seeks further encounters with the whale. The second meeting takes place in a cave in the icy wastes of the Antarctic, where the whales return to their origins after mating. On this occasion "the mother" speaks in a way intelligible to Miriam who manages to record the whale's message only to lose the tape-recorder overboard shortly afterwards. The third and final encounter takes place in the sea of south western Australia when "the mother" is about give birth, while Miriam, too, is pregnant. This primordial elemental tie between the females of two species, so different in genetic terms, yet so close at a psicho-etological level, leads "the mother" and Miriam to finally achieve a mystic telepathetic communication through the mysterious and instinctive bond which links them.

Voyage and quest are key elements in the novel. As in *Il Prato in fondo al mare* there are voyages over and under the sea. The former is undertaken by Nievo the author in two and a half year of travel over the Pacific, Atlantic and Antarctic oceans in his quest for materials for his novel. This experience is transformed in the novel into Miriam's quest for the secret of communication with the whales, which follows essentially the same route. Miriam's journey under the sea, however, has a predominantly metaphysical function. It is not just an extension of her quest for communication represented by her journey on the surface, as the symbiosis achieved by Miriam and "the mother" provides a focus for the quest for the mythical and metaphysical significance of the submarine universe described in the novel. An important element in conveying this is provided by Nievo's narrative technique: part of the story is related from Miriam's point of consciouness; part from that of the whale.

The ocean depths are thus transformed into a place of myth and magic. No longer a place where truth is elusive to the point of unattainability as in *Il Prato in fondo al mare*, the sea becomes a place of revelation and discovery where Miriam finds herself confronted by "the authentic values of life" (De Michelis 1991). Miriam's quest for communication with the whale is also a quest for communication with herself, with her fellow humans, an attempt to achieve an ideal condition where barriers do not exist and all living beings can talk freely to each other, a sort of close encounter with the inhabitants of this planet, rather than with extraterrestrials. It is the hypothesis of an utopian state related to a post-scientific context and achieved not by the use of technical means but through "the warm flux that pulses in the hearts of both creatures" (Toscani 1990). Its attainment responds to an essential and vital need in modern man. As Carlo Sgorlon puts it:

> to communicate is to dissipate the chaos that is in the universe and that is now found especially in humankind; human beings are no longer able to understand each other and write the funereal poetry of alienation. They have come into conflict with life, nature, Being in its totality, and all they can do is cry out their desperation in their rush towards annihilation (Sgorlon 1990).

Nievo suggests that the solution to this dilemma can be found in the bond created between Miriam and "the mother," a total opening up to a communative process arising from "a sort of dream of the origins" (Tesio 1990).

This notion is conveyed particularly in the sequences dedicated to the description of the dream consciousness active in the optic heart of the whale. For the whale, time is circular, past and present are one, dream fuses with memory and both become the same. For humankind time is linear, yet the past does not die easily, indeed it is ever present and self-perpetuating. For women memory is consciousness and so moments such as those experienced by Miriam provide the trigger that dissolves the barrier and consciousness is struck with sudden insight. It is this temporal symbiosis, this granting of reality to the past, that gives the present meaning and prevents humankind from being overcome by the material aspects of existence. The attempt to communicate across the species equates memory with language and the value of language as information.

Miriam's quest explores the very core of existence, taking her where no other contemporary fellow human being has dared to tread and is as much a discovery of self as that of the world of the whales. However, it is also an attempt to explore a common origin with other living species and to recreate this common oneness in the context of a post-scientific world. Finally, there is a quest for perfection: whales are seen as having achieved the peak of evolutionary perfection. But therein lies an unresolved contradiction: their tendency to strand themselves on the beach seems to be due to a mysterious and unconscious urge to return to the land whence they came, an attempt to achieve reunification with human kind.

Stanislao Nievo is a strikingly original new voice in contemporary Italian literature, defying close identification with any particular school or trend. Blending elements of the surreal, the metaphysical and the fantastic, he creates fables which lead to the exploration of "truths" different from those proposed by the rationalistic myopia of the scientific age. His is not the malaise of indifference and *noia* (ennui) which characterizes the existentialist dilemma of modern man posited by many contemporary Italian writers. A man of many interests, ranging from history to ecology, who sees fable and legend as a necessary and vital complement to history and science, Nievo depicts wider and potentially liberating horizons both in a physical and spiritual sense through the exploration of myth, mystery and magic presented from a variety of perspectives, which blend fact and fantasy in the endeavour to penetrate those other worlds which lie beyond apparent reality. In the words of one critic:

> Nievo's new narrative is much more than the statement of an aesthetic conservationalist. If anything it is an enthralling Conradian pilgrimage to the sources of being, of the beginnings of life, of communication, of love (Trotta 1990).

Thus the quest for glimpses of other worlds which Nievo proposes in his narrative works is provided through a kaleidoscope of very different, yet interconnected realities: the primordial world of the New Guinea natives and their ancestors in *Le Isole del paradiso,* that of a different time and place superimposed on a contemporary setting in *Il Palazzo del silenzio* and *Aurora,* the timeless cyclic cosmos of the whales in *The Blue Whale.* These works mark a progressive development from the initial ambiguity of the quest and the nature of its lack of success in *Il Prato in fondo al mare* to the more positive conclusion in *The Blue Whale,* from the figure of the problematic hero in the early novels to the protagonists of *Le Isole del paradiso* and *The Blue Whale,* who in their fashion manage to partially, if not fully, resolve the dilemma posed by life and destiny.[2]

Notes

1 The name has considerable symbolic loading and provides a direct and substantial link to the novel *Aurora.* Miriam – also called Marianne, Marian, Myrrhine, Marina – was an ancient sea goddess, a projection of the archetype of the great mother, empowered with a threefold nature and presiding over birth and growth, battle and love, death and divination. Initially the only power to be worshipped, her cult became less powerful with the advent of patriarchal societies. In Christian mythology she became the Madonna whose predominant colour is blue (Robert Graves, *The White Goddess,* New York: Farrar, Straus & Giroux, 1966, pp. 389, 394-5).

2 These themes are further explored in other works of fiction by Nievo – *Il Tempo del sogno* and *Il Sorriso degli Dei* – published after *The Blue Whale.*

Bibliography

Literary Works by Stanislao Nievo

Il Prato in fondo al mare [Meadow at the Bottom of the Sea], Milan: Mondadori, 1974; Oscar Mondadori ed. 1977 [novel].

Il Padrone della notte [Master of the Night], Milan: Mondadori, 1976; Oscar Mondadori ed. 1988 [short stories].

Viaggio verde [Green Journey], in Mario Forti (ed.), *Almanacco dello specchio*, Milan: Mondadori,1977, pp 274-285 [poetry].

Aurora, Milan, Mondadori, 1979; Oscar Mondadori ed. 1981 [novel].

Il cavallo nero [The Black Horse], Turin: Tirrenia-Stampatori, 1979 [new edition with a different collection of stories: Cinisello Balsamo [Mi]: Edizioni Paoline, 1990] [children's fables].

Il Palazzo del silenzio [Palace of Silence], Milan: Mondadori, 1985 [novel].

Le Isole del paradiso [Islands of Paradise], Milan: Mondadori, 1987 [novel].

Il Pozzo [The Well] in Gabriele la Porta (ed.), *racconti d'incubo,* Roma: Newton Compton Editore, 1988, pp 263-272 [short story].

Canto di Pietra [Song of Stone], Milan: Mondadori, 1989 [Previously published in *Canadian Journal of Italian Studies*, VI: 20-21, Summer-Fall 1982, pp 343-393; contains interview with Nievo, pp 390-393] [poetry].

La Balena azzurra [The Blue Whale], Milan: Mondadori, 1990; Oscar Mondadori ed. 1993 [novel].

La Voragine [The Vortex] in Stanislao Nievo / Maria Clelia Cardona, *La Voragine / La Ricerca del graal*, Naples: Guida, 1991 [short story].

Il Tempo del sogno [Dreamtime], Milan: Mondadori, 1993 [short stories].

Il Sorriso degli Dei [The Smile of the Gods], Venice: Marsilio, 1997 [novel].

Literary Translations by Stanislao Nievo

Rudyard Kypling. *Capitani coraggiosi*. Florence: Giunti Mazzocco, 1988.

Daniel Defoe. *Robinson Crusoe*. Florence: Giunti Mazzocco, 1991.

Translations of Nievo's Literary Works

Il Prato in fondo al mare into Ukranian: Kiev: Vesesvit, 1983; Kiev: Molod, 1986; into Swedish: Stockholm-Rome: Casa Editrice Italica, 1988.

Le Isole del paradiso into French: Paris: Collection 12 Étoiles, 1988.

From *Il Tempo del Sogno* into English: "Dreamtime" in Manfred Jurgensen (ed.), *Riding Out New Writing from Around the World,* Brisbane: Outrider/Phoenix Publications, 1994, pp 403-420.

Selected Criticism up to the Publication of *The Blue Whale*

Amoroso, Giuseppe. "Il romanzo italiano dal 1975 al 1980," *Cultura e Scuola,* XIX, 6 (October-December 1980), pp 34-59.

Anon. "La Balena azzurra," *Tecnologie per il Mare,* December 1990.

Benelli, Gian Carlo. "La balena azzurra," *Abstracta,* December 1990.

Bo, Carlo. "Un signore tenebroso il terremoto di Nievo," *Corriere della Sera,* 17 October 1976.

De Michelis, Cesare. "Con le balene," *Il Gazzettino,* 9 March 1991.

De Turris, Giancarlo. "Stanislao Nievo o il ritorno del mito," in Stanislao Nievo *Il padrone della notte,* Milan: Mondadori [Oscar], 1988, pp 5-24.

Garboli, Cesare. "Introduzione," in Stanislao Nievo, *Il prato in fondo al mare,* Milan: Mondadori [Oscar], 1977, pp 5-11.

Luzi, Mario. "Al canto delle balene," *Il Giornale,* 11 November 1990.

Marabini, Claudio. "Il fantastico esplorare," *Il Resto del Carlino,* 12 May 1987.

Marabini, Claudio. "Introduzione," in Stanislao Nievo, *Aurora,* Milan: Mondadori [Oscar], 1981.

Mattei, Paolo. "La grande madre in fondo al mare," *Il Mattino,* 27 November 1990.

Pasolini, Pier Paolo. "Negli abissi del mare come nell'utero materno," *Il Tempo illustrato,* 1 January 1975.

Sgorlon, Carlo. "Non può mentire (è razza Nievo)," *Il Piccolo,* 22 May 1987.

Sgorlon, Carlo. "Nostra Signora dei Ghiacci," *Il Resto del Carlino,* 13 October 1990.

Tesio, Giovanni. "Cercando la balena nei mari di Nievo," *Tuttolibri*, 20 October 1990.

Toscani, Claudio. "Lo scrittore è un ecologista della parola," *La Provincia*, 11 December 1990.

Toscani, Claudio. "Introduzione," in *La Balena azzurra*, Milan: Mondadori, 1993. pp 1-13.

Trotta, Donatella. "Il paradiso perduto della grande madre," *Il Mattino*, 30 October 1990.